Thi

CONSTABLE AT THE GATE

In the latest collection of tales from Aidensfield, Greengrass and his dog continue their rather dodgy means of earning a living, venturing into the bed-and-breakfast business. A local journalist highlights her devotion to Sergeant Blaketon in her press reports, while Nick copes with village gossips and finds himself searching for old folks who have wandered from home. His action at the scene of a road accident results in a joyful family reunion, while the buyer of a country cottage does not bring much happiness to the constable and people of Aidensfield.

CONSTABLE AT THE GATE

CONSTABLE AT THE GATE

by
Nicholas Rhea

Magna Large Print Books
Long Preston, North Yorkshire,
England.

British Library Cataloguing in Publication Data.

Rhea, Nicholas
  Constable at the gate.

  A catalogue record for this book is
  available from the British Library

  ISBN 0-7505-1273-3

First published in Great Britain by Robert Hale Ltd., 1997

Published in Large Print 1998 by arrangement with Robert Hale Ltd.

Magna Large Print is an imprint of
Library Magna Books Ltd.
Printed and bound in Great Britain by
T.J. International Ltd., Cornwall, PL28 8RW.

Contents

1 Big Gates and Little Gates

The rich man in his castle,
The poor man at his gate,
God made them, high or lowly,
And order'd their estate.
Cecil Frances Alexander (1818–1895)

Aud Willie One-Leg spent his retirement days standing at the small white-painted gate of his modest but very pretty cottage. A semi-detached, stone-built house, it stood—and continues to stand—in the main street of Elsinby, a truly charming village nestling below the hills some two miles from Aidensfield. Elsinby boasts many features, including the splendid Hopbind Inn, a post office, a small but vital village store, a castle which is occupied to this day, a Catholic church and an Anglican church, a primary school, a selection of farms around the extremities and a pretty stream which flows beside the road. That road runs through the centre of this peaceful place as the main street and

9

it is enhanced by rows of rustic cottages.

Aud Willie One-Leg was another of the village features. He could be seen at his gate day in and day out, winter and summer alike. He was like a sentry at his post, determined and diligent in his duty and unflinching in the teeth of autumn gales, winter snows, spring storms and the fly-sticky heat of high summer. He spent very little time indoors; indeed, few had ever set foot inside his cottage—I hadn't.

Like the Yorkshire weather, the seasons changed with remarkable effect but Aud Willie One-Leg never varied in his daily duty—at nine o'clock prompt every morning, Sundays included, he established himself at the gate and remained there until the darkness of the winter evenings enveloped him, or until about five o'clock on the lighter evenings. His daily stint was regulated with breaks for morning coffee, lunch (or dinner as he called it) and a cup of tea in the afternoon; furthermore, he seemed able to arrange his toilet necessities to coincide with his official breaks. Willie's devotion to duty and the timing of his daily task meant that everyone living nearby knew what time he would make his appearance. As one man said, 'You can set your clock by Aud Willie.'

Willie was in his late seventies and his real name was William Watson; he was a widower, his devoted wife, Edith, having died some ten years earlier. A stocky man of middle height, he possessed hands like shovels, a round, weathered and rather whiskery face out of which sprouted a moustache. He had grizzly grey hair which poked unceremoniously from beneath his cap, and strikingly blue eyes, yet I'd never seen him wearing spectacles. He always wore the same dull brown flat cap, tweed jacket with leather around the cuffs and elbows, and brown corduroy trousers.

Those well-worn trousers concealed his false leg. That he had a false leg became evident as he stomped about the village or went across to the Hopbind Inn for his nightly couple of pints, but for his daily sentinel duty, one would never have realized he had such a handicap—unless one approached him for a chat. If that happened, he'd explain in graphic detail how he'd lost his leg.

But for his daily responsibilities, however, he removed the false leg and folded the bottom half of his right trouser leg up behind his thigh where it was held in position with a colossal safety pin. During the day's guard duties, therefore, he relied on a small shelf which he had fashioned at precisely the correct height on the inside of his gate. He rested the stump of his leg on that shelf and was able to lean on the gatepost with his arm across the top, a position which he assured everyone was infinitely more comfortable than standing all day on a false leg.

Another facet of Willie's character was that his dress never varied throughout the year, his only concession being to wear a thick overcoat and a scarf when the really ferocious weather of winter set in or to open a huge and highly colourful golfing umbrella if it rained heavily. The umbrella was a gift from one of his fans—for Willie did have his fans. Regular visitors to Elsinby pointed him out to their friends and I do know that some drove out from places like York and Ripon to see him at his gate. In his own way, Aud Willie One-Leg had become a tourist attraction.

Willie's entire working life had been spent at High Leas, a thriving farm in the hills behind the village. His only break was a spell of active service in the army during the First World War. He had fought in the trenches in France and, at the age of twenty-five, he'd got in the way of a shell, so he told everyone, and had lost his right leg below the knee. His stump had been fitted with a wooden shaft and this had never seemed to hamper his work on the farm where he milked the cows, fed the pigs, looked after the poultry and did every other feasible job from maintaining the plough to somehow managing to drive the tractor.

There was no doubt that Willie had been a veritable treasure to generations of the family which had farmed at High Leas. He'd worked for a succession of masters, always without complaint but with total loyalty and, as a reward, he had the occupancy of Jasmine Cottage for the tiniest of rents. He could remain there until his death and he was very content, so he told everyone.

It was his false leg which had given him the name of Aud Willie One-Leg. Aud, pronounced *ord* in the North Riding of Yorkshire, is a term of affection and although it can be translated as meaning 'old', it is not generally used as a reflection of a person's age. Instead, it is a term of esteem and affection, often used to refer to both men and animals—a beloved dog will be Aud Ben or Aud Rover, a favourite cow will be Aud Lass or Aud Primrose, and a beloved wife of any age will be My Aud Woman—and so it was that William Watson was known to all the local people as Aud Willie One-Leg.

His cottage was built of the local tan-coloured limestone with a red pantile roof and, in keeping with the traditional image of such a place, it had roses around the rustic archway which stood around the door and honeysuckle climbing over the solitary outbuilding—which was, in fact, the outside toilet. Indeed, it was the only toilet. It was a very attractive cottage, beautifully maintained with white-painted woodwork and fronted by a neat white gate bearing its name. There were well-tended borders around a small, tidily trimmed lawn too, all the work of Willie who tended his little plot when he was not standing on guard at the gate.

In addition to its rustic charm, the cottage was very strategically placed for Willie's purpose. It was on Elsinby's main street and almost opposite the Hopbind Inn; the post office was just around the corner to the right, with the school just up the lane to his left; the entrance to the castle lay about a hundred yards along the street, only a few yards from the shop. The two churches, always busy with visitors, cleaners, flower-arrangers and others, not to mention Sunday services, weddings, baptisms and funerals, were situated just off that main street too. The fortuitous positioning of those strategic village institutions meant that Aud Willie One-Leg was never short of someone to talk to. In fact, he was at the centre of activities, a focal point for the community in much the same way as the war memorial or village pump. Almost everyone who walked along that short main street was within hailing distance of Willie as he mounted guard at Jasmine Cottage. And hail them he did, strangers and locals alike. If a visitor was walking along the street full of admiration for the charms of the place, or perhaps heading into the pub for a pint of cool beer or a quiet lunch, Willie would call out, 'It's a grand day!' or 'It's not a very nice day', his opening gambit depending upon the state of the prevailing weather conditions.

People from the south of England

were somewhat unnerved by this show of friendship for they were not, and are not, accustomed to speaking to total strangers let alone be bidden the time of day by a Yorkshireman in a flat cap. But most would respond by agreeing with Willie.

'Yes, it's a very nice day,' they would say, or 'No, it's not very pleasant.' Some would just nod their heads or wave in agreement.

'It's not as good as it was yesterday but mebbe it's better than it'll be tomorrow,' was a typical Willie response, alternating with, 'Bad days come and go, and it'll get better in time. However bad it is, there's allus worse somewhere else.'

'Yes, I suppose so,' and many townies, believing that Yorkshire country folk with rosy cheeks can forecast the weather by looking at birds, bees and weeds or sniffing the air would then say, 'I'm on holiday, and I do hope the weather is going to be kind.'

'You are in Yorkshire, think on,' would be Willie's wry reply, his form of warning about the unexpected climatic conditions on the remote moors. 'Compared wi' t'climate down south, they reckon it's allus bit chilly up here, but some folks

16

can't abide good aud-fashioned fresh air. That's all it is—good, pure fresh air. But I reckon you'll not be disappointed—so long as you take a raincoat with you.'

And so the visitor would be hooked. Once Willie had ensnared him, he'd be there for an hour or more, listening to tales of how Willie's leg had been blown off by a shell and how he once milked the entire herd in the middle of the field because a whirlwind had flattened the milking parlour. He told a good story, did Willie, and his summer days passed in the entertainment of unsuspecting tourists. Many went home thinking he typified the rustics of North Yorkshire but in fact he was unique.

The locals, however, tried to avoid him, not because they disliked him but because if he managed to catch any of them passing by, it meant at least an hour was lost. In some cases, his conversation was like a constantly running tape—he repeated the same yarn time and time again.

Sadly, few of them had the time that was needed to listen to his ramblings but to listen to them repeatedly was definitely quite boring. In their efforts to avoid being caught by Willie, the people of

Elsinby would watch through their cottage windows and wait until he, like a spider, had caught some other unfortunate person in his web, preferably a tourist.

At that point, they would all rush into the village, to do their bits of shopping, post office visiting, church cleaning, calling on friends or nipping into the Hopbind for a pint. But woe betide anyone who was the first down that street on any morning of the week ... like the spider waiting for the fly, Willie was waiting.

I did wonder whether the residents of Elsinby had thought of devising a rota system of outings which would allocate to a volunteer the task of being first on to the street on a given morning. I do know there was talk about it in the pub from time to time. It would work something like this—if Mrs Brown ventured out first on Monday, with Mr Kenton on Tuesday, the Misses Hindmarsh on Wednesdays and so on through the week, it would relieve the pressure on everyone. Knowing that the first person to venture out after nine o'clock would inevitably be hailed by Willie, it seemed a good idea to apportion that task to a different volunteer for each day. Everyone in the village could take

18

a turn—but that scheme never came to fruition. It seemed everyone preferred to avoid Willie if at all possible and it was quite true that many of the locals relied on visitors for their salvation; after all, Elsinby was a pretty place often resorted to by trippers from nearby towns and cities and if they heard Willie only once, it presented hope to the local people.

So far as Willie was concerned, such visitors were a godsend, strangers were welcomed and business people seeking addresses in the village were wonderful because each was caught by Willie and this allowed the village to go about its normal business.

For me, of course, as the village constable, Willie was priceless. He was the eyes and ears of Elsinby, he saw everything and everyone, he knew everything that was happening in the place and he loved to talk. One might have regarded him as a perfect witness but this was not the case. Apart from the problem of getting away from him once he started to tell his story, the other problem was that he never actually told me anything—in spite of diligent efforts on my part. I feel sure he *thought* he had imparted to me some great

19

and important crime-fighting news but this was rarely the case.

In dealing with Willie, however, I had to be constantly aware of the passing time for I could not afford the luxury of standing around and gossiping all day. Unlike most of the locals, however, I had an excuse to tear myself away from his tale-telling by stating I had an urgent appointment or a vital professional meeting with Sergeant Blaketon or some other senior officer. In some instances, of course, I simply motored past without stopping, albeit with a friendly wave, but I never ignored him.

I was soon to learn that one of his strengths—or perhaps it was a ploy—was to associate his tales with the person to whom he was conversing—Doctor William Williams, for example, was regaled with tales of how Willie's missing leg still ached while the plumber heard stories about non-existent hot-and-cold water in the trenches; the district nurse was told of life in military hospitals while the vicar was tested on his knowledge of the Bible, Willie having swotted his piece the previous evening. Farmers of the modern generation were told how it used to be in Willie's time, how the corn was cut with scythe and how milk from old-fashioned churns tasted better than the newfangled heat-treated stuff. And so it went on, with Willie gaining knowledge about everything and everyone. Whenever he talked to me, though, it was the outrageous lawlessness of some of the Elsinby residents which formed his subject matter.

'You ought to do summat about that lad with his motor bike,' he would say out of the corner of his mouth, as if imparting a major secret.

'What lad?' I would ask.

'Thoo knows! Him from up yonder.' And he would attempt to indicate some vague direction with a slight movement of his head, doubtless not wanting himself to be considered a police informant by giving too much away.

After several futile and unproductive attempts to draw from him the name or even the address of this grievous offender, I would ask, 'So, what's he done? This motor cyclist?'

'Well, thoo's t'bobby, thoo should know!'

'Yes, Willie, but if I don't know *who* you're talking about ...'

'Now it's not for me to say things about other folks, as thoo well knows, but summat'll have to be done. What's good for t'goose is good for t'gander.'

'Is he driving without a licence?' I would ask. 'Or driving his bike when he's under age, maybe?'

'Now, it's not in my nature to tell tales, Mr Rhea, but thoo should know what's going on in this place. Then if thoo knows what's going on, thoo can do summat about it, and mebbe put a stop to it. That's what I say.'

'Yes, that makes sense,' I would agree. 'So what's he up to, this motor cyclist? What is it that I should be stopping?'

'Well, I hope you soon find out and do summat about it because it's not good for him, and it's not good for others, Mr Rhea, mark my words. But if I was thoo, I'd keep my eyes open and then you'll be able to do summat to stop it all.'

'Yes, I will,' I assured him but with absolutely no idea who or what he was talking about. Certainly, there were lads with motor bikes in the village but none could be regarded a nuisance. Some enjoyed scrambling, the term we used for riding over the rough moorland with specially adapted machines, while others were content to use their bikes as a means of transport or as a magnet for attracting girl-friends. But I knew none who was misbehaving and was blissfully unable to draw from Willie the precise nature of his complaint or information, nor did I ever obtain a name of the supposed villain.

Very quickly, I began to realize this was one of his tactics. He would impart his own brand of knowledge to me, somehow managing to define his own boundaries as to whether he was acting with spite as a police informer or being a noble guardian of the peace in Elsinby.

To quote another example, with a wave and a shout he hailed me one morning as I was heading towards the Hopbind Inn to discuss with the landlord his application for an occasional licence. I had a few minutes in hand, and thinking I might be about to receive some vital crime-busting information, I halted for a chat with Willie. It was a hot day in August with not a cloud in the sky.

'Now then, Willie,' I gave the traditional Yorkshire greeting.

'Now then, Mr Rhea,' he moved his head in acknowledgement. 'Not a bad day but mebbe a bit on t'warm side. I've known worse and I've known hotter, but it's not as hot as that day our beck dried up ... you'll remember that, Mr Rhea? Nay, it was before your time ...'

'You wanted to see me?' I had to direct him to the matter he wished to discuss, otherwise I should never be told anything useful.

'Aye, I'm glad I caught you.' He looked right and left as if making sure no one else was eavesdropping upon our conversation.

There was no one in the street at that moment, although within seconds, two doors of nearby houses opened and two ladies sailed forth towards the shop. Mrs Charlton and Mrs Beeforth were both glad that someone was occupying Willie—they'd been waiting for this moment all morning and with a bit of luck, they could complete their trips and get back into their homes before Willie had finished with me. But it would be touch and go, as I knew my own time was very limited.

'What's the problem?' I put to him.

'It's that lad from them new houses,' he almost whispered the words.

'Which lad?' I asked.

'You know, him whose dad was badly recently, had to go to hospital, gall stones or summat, his dad I mean, him with that

24

old black car. Well, it's his lad.'

'What's his name? The son, I mean,' I asked without much hope of a positive answer.

'You should know that, Mr Rhea, I shouldn't be surprised if it's in your records somewhere. Funny family, they are, allus up to no good. They're from Middlesbrough or is it Stockton? You'll know that of course.'

'So, this lad. What's he been up to?' I asked.

'Well, you should know that, Mr Rhea! I'm right surprised at you asking me that one!'

'So why did you want to tell me about him?'

'Well, I thought you and your mates had mebbe better keep an eye on him, you know.'

'Really? Why?'

'Well, you know what he's up to!'

'I don't, if I'm honest,' I said.

'Well, all this coming and going, out at all hours ...'

'Probably it's because he's got a girl-friend,' I suggested.

'Has he, by Jove? I never knew that! You're one jump ahead of them there,

Mr Rhea. So do you know him ...'

'No, I was just suggesting that if a young man stays out late, it's a fair indication he's got himself a girl-friend. It's often nothing more sinister than that; it doesn't mean he's a burglar,' I tried to explain.

'No young woman in her right mind would touch him with a barge-pole.' He shook his old head as if imparting some great wisdom. 'Not with a barge-pole. But I thought I'd better mention it.'

'You did right.' I looked at my watch. There was literally a couple of minutes before my meeting with George Ward at the pub. 'Now I must be off, Willie. Thanks for the chat!'

I managed to detach myself from him without a lot of trouble because I had seen the two ladies returning from the shop—Willie had got his eye on them and I knew he preferred talking to ladies. Leaving him, I crossed the quiet road and within minutes, was settling down with George over a mug of coffee. Through the window of George's private accommodation, I could see that Willie had managed to waylay one of the homeward bound ladies, Mrs Charlton.

'I reckon Charlie Charlton's going to

26

have a late dinner,' commented George.

It was several days later when I read in my evening paper that an Elsinby man, Ian Hebditch, aged twenty-two, had been convicted at York Magistrates Court of driving his father's car without the necessary insurance. The vehicle had been insured for the policyholder only—i.e. dad, not for all drivers and certainly not for lads under twenty-five years of age.

Ian's address was given as No. 18, Beckside Cottages and his occupation was painter and decorator. In court, he'd apologized for the lapse and said his motor bike had failed to start that morning and he'd borrowed his father's car at short notice to get to work; the problem of insurance had never occurred to him and it was an innocent mistake. He'd been stopped on the outskirts of York by a traffic policeman but the court treated him leniently; he was fined £5 and had his licence endorsed.

Two or three days later, I was back in Elsinby when Aud Willie One-Leg hailed me once more.

'By gum, Mr Rhea, you acted fast on that tip-off I gave you.'

'Did I?' For the moment, I was puzzled by my success.

'Driving without insurance, eh? Nasty business, Mr Rhea, I knew he was up to no good. Lads with motor bikes need watching, Mr Rhea, as you well know, especially when they're out at all hours. Now, there's that chap up yonder ...'

And he jerked his head in some rather unspecific direction.

'Which chap?' I decided to go along with him now. Clearly, Willie thought I was acting upon his gems of crime-busting information.

'Lives in that caravan up by Howe Plantation ... now, he's up to summat, mark my words.'

'I'll keep an eye open!' I promised.

'And so will I,' he assured me.

And so the crime-busting team of Rhea and Aud Willie One-Leg was formed.

But I never asked him to give evidence in court—I had the feeling he would confuse the magistrates.

There was another interesting gate which I motored past almost every day of my police duty. It was called Waterloo Gate and stood on a junction at a noted and potentially dangerous corner of the main road which led into Ashfordly from Harrowby. It was at that junction that the minor road for Aidensfield and Briggsby joined the main road. The corner featured frequently in traffic accidents, particularly during the winter months when the combination of a very sharp bend, an adverse camber and icy conditions caused vehicles to leave the road or collide with each other. In the course of my work, I had dealt with several spills at that point, happily none of them fatal.

In all cases, my dealings were overshadowed by the magnificent gate. It had been erected in 1818 at the entrance to Briggsby Lodge which lay hidden in woods just off that corner and commemorated the Duke of Wellington's defeat of Napoleon at the Battle of Waterloo in 1815. Some said the gate had been erected by descendants of Wellington, others claimed it was the work of local survivors of that historic contest and yet more said it had been paid for by the occupants of the big house which stood some distance behind it. Whatever its origins, it comprised two tall and sturdy stone pillars with a graceful stone arch linking them at the top, and a pair of handsome iron gates which would not have looked out of place at the entrance to Buckingham Palace.

In the space above the gates and in the hollow centre of the arch, there was an heraldic crest painted in gold, silver, white, red, blue and yellow. It was secured to a series of iron bars which matched the gates beneath and bore the single word 'Vorwarts'.

Briggsby Lodge, set in the modest parklands behind the gate, was a small Palladian mansion and, like Aud Willie One-Leg's home, this was one place I had never entered during my period as the village constable of Aidensfield. In fact, the house itself stood just over the boundaries of my beat although its splendid gate was on my patch; the house lay within the jurisdiction of Ashfordly Section, and was thus within the care of Sergeant Blaketon and the officers of that market town.

Nothing had ever occurred which would require me to visit the house on duty but in fact, the occupant was a recluse called Gertrude Fossard who was never seen out of the building and who never invited anyone in. The exception was one local lady, Miss Helen Glanville of Briggsby, who did her cleaning, washing, shopping, general administration of the house and the running of errands. She organized men to care for the grounds and parkland, saw that some of it was rented for grazing and permitted a local farmer to grow potatoes in a distant corner. All this ensured that Miss Fossard had an additional income from her land, and that the grounds of her house were well maintained.

The busy Miss Glanville, a large, red-haired lady in her fifties, cycled from her home to the Lodge almost every day and I understand she was paid well for her devotion to the recluse.

In time, I learned that Miss Gertrude Fossard was a lady of independent means in her late seventies. She claimed ancestry dating to Norman times—certainly, down the centuries, the Fossards had been noted landowners in the North Riding with castles and estates at Whorlton and elsewhere, along with historic links to the English sovereigns and to Parliament itself, but I had no idea whether or not her ancestral claims were true. I knew of no other Fossards in the area; most certainly, it was no longer a plentiful name among the county's aristocracy.

Miss Fossard was just one of many aristocrats who lived upon or nearby my patch at Aidensfield and, unless her house was raided by housebreakers, burglars or confidence tricksters, there was no reason for me to pay her a call. She never left the house and so it was never empty and therefore never required my supervision as unoccupied premises. That was a service we offered to those who left their homes empty for extended or even short periods.

In spite of a lack of specific requests for police attention, I felt sure the Ashfordly constables would be keeping the house and grounds under careful scrutiny for malefactors; consequently the life and times of Miss Gertrude Fossard were relegated to the back of my mind. She caused no problems and demanded no attention from the police as she lived quietly in her splendid mansion behind the beautiful Waterloo Gate. The gate, in fact, was not used as the regular entrance to the house, although Miss Glanville on her bicycle took a short cut via that route. Other visiting traffic such as the butcher's van or tradesmen, used another entrance which emerged in Ashfordly, not far from the market-place.

It meant, in general terms, that Waterloo Gate was more of a showpiece than an actual gateway, the route from there to the mansion being little more than an unsurfaced track through the parkland.

One dark and wintry Saturday morning in January, with northerly winds causing icy patches and flurries of snow creating drifts on some of our more exposed roads, the life of Miss Fossard was far from my mind as I patrolled the outer regions of my beat in my official Mini-van. And then I received a radio message. It came from PC Alf Ventress at Ashfordly Police Station.

'Nick,' he said after I had responded to the call sign, 'what's your location?'

'Briggsby,' I said. 'Just leaving High Curragh Farm.'

'Good.' There was a note of relief in his voice. 'We've just received a report of an accident at Waterloo Gate. One vehicle involved, driver injured. Can you attend? Alwyn Foxton can't go, he's dealing with a sudden death.'

'I'm on my way!' I responded. 'Has the ambulance been called?'

'Yes, it's on its way. ETA—ten minutes.'

'I'll be there in five minutes,' I told him, signing off the air.

Wary of the prevailing road conditions and carefully negotiating the drifts—known locally as stowerings—which were formed as the light snow was blown through gaps in the bare hedgerows, I made my way to Waterloo Gate. When I arrived, I discovered a red Hillman Minx had collided with the sturdy left pillar of Waterloo Gate.

It had apparently skidded on black ice on the corner, left the road, hurtled over a wide grassy verge and then come to a violent halt against the strength of the pillar at the left of the gate. The gates themselves were open, probably the result of the impact, but they did not appear to be damaged. A young man was in the car, slumped over the steering wheel, and I noted the ominous patch of red on the remains of the shattered windscreen. I knew he would have head and facial injuries. A young farmer and his dog were standing nearby, anxiously awaiting my approach. I recognized him as Jim Atkinson.

'You called the police, Jim?' I asked.

'Aye, from t'house,' he said. I knew he lived near the junction. 'Ah 'eard this bang and came out, Ah dossn't move him.'

'No, you did right to leave him. The ambulance is coming,' I said. 'Now, let's have a look at him.'

The impact with the huge stones of the gate had crushed the front of the car, curling the metal of its bonnet and wings until they looked like shavings from a piece of wood. This had exposed the innards and the engine. I could also see some damage to the stonework of the gate pillar, but was unable to make a full assessment with the car in its present position. The driver was lying very still in the wreckage of his car, his chest against the steering wheel and his bleeding head resting against the windscreen. The blood was not spurting, I noted with relief, so he hadn't burst an artery. That knowledge considerably reduced the urgency of the situation. The driver's door was wide open, flung wide by the impact. I spoke to him.

There was no reply. I touched him. He was warm, alive I felt, but clearly in need of urgent medical attention. That head wound could prove serious and he might have done some damage to his ribs and lungs. A broken rib could pierce a lung in these circumstances, but I knew better than move him—first aid was suitable in some cases, but our training had taught me that head and chest injuries should be left to the experts.

I made sure the car's ignition was switched off and that there was no danger from fire, then searched his pockets for documents which might identify him. I found nothing but a small leather wallet which contained £50 in notes and some loose change. I replaced it, wondering who he was; certainly, he was a stranger to me. By the time I had undertaken all my checks to see if the driver was trapped or whether his legs and arms were broken, the ambulance arrived from Brantsford.

After a quick appraisal of the situation, the two ambulance men with my assistance withdrew the injured man from the wreckage, placed him on the stretcher along with his holdall of personal belongings and, within seconds, he was speeding towards Brantsford Memorial Hospital. I was left with the car to deal with and a lot of paperwork to complete. Jim Atkinson had remained throughout, scattering grit with a shovel from my Mini-van and telling a handful of passing motorists who stopped that help was coming. He politely suggested they didn't cause further obstructions or increase the risk of further accidents on the icy surface. Jim was of enormous help to me during those busy moments. Fortunately, the falling snow was not very heavy, now reduced to a gentle scattering of flakes.

Even so, it was continuing to drift in the more exposed regions. After I had taken the necessary details of the car such as its make, model, date of manufacture and registration number, including a brief note of its damage, and then taken measurements of the scene along with the relative position of the car, I radioed Alf Ventress and asked him to arrange for a breakdown truck to tow it to Aidensfield Garage. There, it would be subjected to a closer scrutiny, such as tests on its brakes and steering, and then left for disposal by the company which had insured it. I searched the car for any further personal belongings of the driver or any valuables which I should have to take into safe-keeping pending their return to him, but there was nothing apart from a tool kit and spare wheel. I found nothing which provided his name or address, and his holdall had gone to hospital with him.

It was while awaiting the arrival of

the breakdown truck that I noticed Miss Glanville pushing her cycle from the Lodge along the snow-covered track towards Waterloo Gate. Clearly, her daily stint at Briggsby Lodge was over for the day, and her arrival was fortuitous—I could inform her of the damage and ask her to notify her employer. I hailed her as she approached the gate, sensibly clad in a heavy overcoat and wellington boots.

'Hello, Mr Rhea.' She spoke in the broad manner of the rural folk in this region. 'Trouble, is it?'

'This car skidded and hit the gate post,' I pointed to the damage. 'The driver's in Brantsford Hospital but at this stage I don't know his condition or even his name. Anyway, he'll be interviewed in due course, and his insurance company will have to be notified about the damage to Miss Fossard's gate. I'm not sure how badly damaged the gatepost is at this stage, but I'll know once the car is removed, and then I'll provide Miss Fossard with details of the insurer when I know them. Perhaps she will contact them direct, to claim the cost of the repair?'

'Yes, all right. I'll tell her when I go back later this evening. Is the driver badly hurt? She may like to know.'

'He had injuries to his head, but he was not dead,' I told her. 'I'll let you know the moment I have some more detailed news. You're going back tonight, in this weather?'

'It's only a half-hour walk across the park, Mr Rhea, and I can stay the night if I want. She likes me to keep her company at dinner and to be honest, I quite enjoy it myself. I do live alone, you see ...'

'It's kind of you,' I said. 'But I don't think the damage to the gate is very serious.'

And I watched as she decided not to mount her trusty cycle for the final half-mile home, instead choosing to wheel it through the light covering of snow. Some ninety minutes later, the breakdown truck towed the wrecked car backwards from its resting place against the pillar and it was only then that I could see the damage to the stonework. The two large stones which had absorbed most of the impact had been dislodged and I could now see they were a few inches out of true and would have to be realigned.

The pillar was certainly in no danger of falling down and the stones were not supporting the hinges of the gate, consequently the gate itself and its surrounding metalwork had not suffered. I noted the extent of the damage in my pocket book, and it would be entered in my official report of the accident, an abstract of which would eventually be sent to the driver's insurance company. Miss Fossard would probably wish to recover the cost of repairs from them and I felt she would have no difficulty with her claim.

Once the scene was clear, I thanked Jim Atkinson for his help, climbed into my van and headed for home, providing via my radio an update of the situation for Alf Ventress at Ashfordly Police Station. At home, my first task was to discover the condition and identity of the driver; relatives would have to be informed and, once he was well enough, he would have to be interviewed for his version of the accident. And I would have to formally notify the owner of the damaged gatepost about details of the driver's insurance. The compilation of a routine report about a road traffic accident involved a lot of careful and detailed preparatory work followed by a lot of office work. But that was my job.

From my home, I rang Brantsford Hospital and asked for Casualty.

'It's PC Rhea from Aidensfield,' I announced, and then explained about the accident and its victim. 'He was brought in earlier this morning. I'm ringing about his condition, and hopefully to get a name and address.'

'He is still unconscious, Mr Rhea,' the ward sister told me. 'Can you call back?'

'Yes, of course. But did you search his clothes? I wondered if he carried any documents which would identify him? I checked but found nothing.'

'No, we didn't find anything either. He has a wallet with fifty pounds or so in it, but nothing to say who he is. No driving licence or anything. There's a bag too, with some overnight things in it, but no name there either. You'll be checking through his car registration, will you? Perhaps you'd let us know?'

'It's Saturday,' I said. 'The taxation department will be closed until Monday, so I can't check his car registration number.'

If it was urgent, however, I could ask a police officer from Northallerton town patrol to let himself into the vehicle taxation department of County Hall from

41

where he could obtain details of the registered owner. In practice, though, this procedure had to be used only in an emergency. I explained this to the nurse who said, 'Well, to be honest, we don't think his injuries are life threatening. He has been examined by a doctor; his lungs and chest are severely bruised but there is no serious damage, and his head wound comprises lacerations, not a fractured skull. He is not severely injured, Mr Rhea, and could recover consciousness before too long.'

'Well, that's good news. Look, call me if things change; in the meantime, I will circulate the number among my colleagues in case anyone recognizes it, and if things change and you think we need to trace relatives urgently, I'll get someone to visit taxation.'

There were no clear rules about what constituted an 'emergency' in such cases, but the employees of the taxation department were never very happy about policemen entering the place during their absence, thus we had to exercise some discretion about the frequency of these visits and the resultant searching of their records. I decided to wait to see if the casualty regained consciousness—and, of course, it was perfectly feasible that someone might start worrying about his non-arrival and ring us for information. For that reason, I passed details of the accident and the registration number of the car to our control room at force headquarters—just in case anxious relatives rang to ask if we knew anything of the red Hillman and its driver.

It would be around 4.30 when I received a call from Brantsford Hospital to say that the car driver had recovered consciousness—but he couldn't remember anything about the accident, and he had no idea who he was, where he'd come from or where he was heading. His medical condition, however, was very good—although injured in the crash, his injuries were not life threatening and he could be expected to leave hospital by the middle of next week. But he had no idea where he would go. I decided this was an emergency, and that a constable should visit the taxation department to provide me with the name of the owner of the red Hillman.

Accordingly, I rang Northallerton town office and spoke to the duty sergeant, explaining the situation, and he agreed with me. He would send someone around straight away and would ring me back within the hour. He did—and I received a surprise.

The owner of the red Hillman was Nigel Fossard, and his address was given as Kirkcross Hall, Kirkcross in Cumberland. It didn't take a genius to work out that the young man had been on his way to meet Gertrude Fossard at Briggsby Lodge, and yet Miss Glanville had never mentioned his expected arrival—even if he'd almost knocked the gate down in his attempt to reach the house. The small amount of luggage in his car suggested his stay would be a short one, so I rang Miss Glanville at her home, but got no reply. She'd already gone to Briggsby Lodge, I guessed, and I decided to contact her there. I peered outside in the darkness; the snow had eased by now. In fact, none had fallen since lunchtime and so the roads were quite safe and a slight increase in temperature had removed any ice. Rather than ring Miss Fossard, therefore, I decided to make a personal visit.

When I rang the huge bell at the door to Briggsby Lodge, a light was switched on above the porch and Miss Glanville emerged to greet me.

'Oh, hello, Mr Rhea. Look, come in, please. It's cold out there.'

She led me into the hall with its giant grandfather clock, suits of armour and family portraits along the walls.

'Miss Glanville,' I said. 'You remember this morning's accident, at the gate?'

She smiled. 'You're going to say the damage is worse than expected! I did tell Miss Fossard, by the way.'

'Well, yes, it was rather more serious than I had first realized, but that isn't the reason for my visit. It's the young man who was hurt: it's possible he was on his way here, to see Miss Fossard.'

'Really? But she wasn't expecting anyone, she does not have visitors. What makes you think he was coming here?'

'His name is Nigel Fossard,' I said, and provided the address, adding, 'He's recovered consciousness in hospital, but has lost his memory. Now, I haven't interviewed him yet but I am assured he is not seriously hurt.'

'I don't know what to say, Mr Rhea. She has never mentioned any other person in her family, all the time I've known her.

I've always thought she was the last of the line ... but I didn't pry, you understand.'

I was rapidly trying to decide whether or not to tell Miss Fossard, when I heard a female voice call, 'Who is it, Helen? At this time of night ... what's the matter?' A tall, rather gaunt lady materialized from the shadows at the distant end of the hall and pottered towards us with the aid of a walking stick.

'Perhaps Mr Rhea would like to explain?' Helen Glanville invited.

'Then don't leave him standing there, take him into the library, there's a fire and I would imagine he'd like something warm to drink!'

I was agreeably surprised by the warmth of her reception and wondered if I had blundered by assuming the accident victim was a member of her family, but I knew I must explain my thoughts to her. Her idea of something warm to drink was a malt whisky and although I was on duty, I decided that one measure would not adversely affect my driving.

'So, Constable.' She smiled sweetly. 'You have news for me?'

I began by recounting the collision with Waterloo Gate and briefly explained the extent of the damage, following with the hospital's efforts, and mine, to identify the driver, albeit not giving his name at this stage. I did add, however, that he had apparently lost his memory.

'It's a bit embarrassing,' I went on. 'Because I assumed he was coming here to see you, but Miss Glanville says you were not expecting anyone.'

'And why should you have thought that, Constable? I do not get many visitors.'

'His name is Fossard,' I told her. 'Nigel Fossard,' and I added his address.

She sat in stunned silence for a long time as I sipped from my glass, then she said, 'Constable, I had no idea there were any Fossards left. You must take me to visit this young man.'

'Now?' I suggested.

'Yes, now. We may use your transport?'

'It's a small van,' I began.

'I wouldn't care if it was a motor bike and sidecar,' she said. 'Come, let's get on with it!'

And so, to my surprise, and to the astonishment of Miss Glanville, Miss Fossard donned a warm fur coat, boots and hat, and plonked herself in the somewhat cramped passenger seat of my tiny Mini-van. During our drive to the hospital, a mere quarter of an hour, she explained she hadn't been out of the house for years because there had been no reason to do so.

Now, though, there was reason enough to break with that self-imposed routine. When we arrived, I explained to the ward sister what had happened and she said, 'Yes, you can see him. He is conscious, but still has no recollection of the accident.'

We were led to the bedside of a dark-haired young man who was dressed in hospital pyjamas and who lay with a huge bandage around his head and a couple of truly memorable black eyes. It looked as if he'd done fifteen rounds with the world heavyweight champion, Cassius Clay. He frowned at our approach, first staring at my uniform, and then at the fur-clad lady at my side.

'He's a Fossard!' she told me. 'I'd know that chin anywhere ... hello, young man. My name is Fossard. Gertrude Fossard from Briggsby. I think you must be a kinsman ... now, we can't have you lying here with no visitors and I want you to regain your memory. Now, which Fossard are you?'

'I'm sorry,' he said. 'I can't remember anything ... I don't know who I am or where I'm from or why I'm here like this ...'

'Then I shall make it my job to make sure you do remember,' she said. 'We can't have a Fossard losing his memory. Now, Constable, can you leave me with him for a while? Get yourself a cup of tea or something, then you can take me home.'

To cut short a long story, Nigel turned out to be a distant relative of Gertrude but one whose relationship had been lost or forgotten with the passage of time, family disasters, ancient feuds, long bouts of non-communication and other factors. In time, he did recall his personal details yet he never regained any memory of that accident—but he did visit Miss Fossard at Briggsby Lodge.

Quite suddenly, the lady who thought she was the last of a long line of Fossards came to realize she was not alone in the world. From being a recluse with no one to think about, Gertrude now had a family.

I learned he had not been travelling to visit her—he'd had no idea of her existence either. He had been *en route* to see his

49

girl-friend who lived near Scarborough, but she had not raised the alarm because she wasn't expecting him that weekend. He'd intended his visit to be a surprise.

But a couple of years later, Gertrude was invited to their wedding, and then, a further two years later, she was invited to be godmother to their baby—Joan Gertrude, both family names of generations of Fossards.

And all because of a patch of ice at Waterloo Gate.

2 Words Speak Louder

Report me and my cause aright.
William Shakespeare (1564–1616)

During the 1960s, relations between the Press and the police were like two feuding sisters—they didn't speak unless it was absolutely necessary and even when they did, there was some suspicion on both sides. The police often felt the Press would resort to sensationalism rather than honest reportage in order to sell newspapers, while the Press seemed to nurse a perpetual notion that the police were hiding something which, in their opinion, should be made public. In most cases, both were wrong. The Press, particularly local newspapers, did want to print good wholesome stories about police work and the police did not deliberately conceal matters of public interest. The root of the problem was that there was no formal police procedure for providing the Press with official newsworthy items.

During that time, few, if any, police forces had an official Press officer to speak on their behalf, and because police regulations stipulated that officers must not pass information to the Press, radio or television, it meant that any news gleaned from the police about internal or official matters was often gathered by subterfuge or cunning rather than through open dialogue. This led to distortions of the truth but it must be said that the reluctance of the police to inform the Press about their work was rather short-sighted and it did create problems.

A high percentage of police work directly involves the public, thus constructive reporting of aspects of it can improve relations between the people and their police service, and consequently build confidence between them. It is difficult to understand why this was not appreciated in the past. On the other hand, it must not be forgotten that a great deal of police work is of a necessarily confidential nature which means that the Press and the public cannot and should not be acquainted with everything undertaken by police officers. Some secrets must be maintained.

The unfortunate situation was that

quite often it was secretive or sensitive information that was hunted by reporters, found by various ruses and then splashed across the pages of the less savoury newspapers. Somewhere between total secrecy and absolute openness, there was room for a controlled flow of positive, sensible and useful news.

When I was the constable at Aidensfield in the 1960s, chief constables throughout the country were beginning to realize that the Press could help the police in much of their work—community relations and crime prevention were just two examples. Things were changing if only very slowly and my first intimation of a more open relationship with the Press came with a telephone call from Sergeant Blaketon.

'Rhea,' he announced one morning after asking if all was quiet on my beat, 'you have been especially selected for a very important, high-profile and innovative duty. The chief constable in person has approved your selection for this task, so you'd better make sure you make a good job of it.'

Wondering what I had been volunteered to do, I asked, 'Well, I'll do my best, Sergeant. So what am I to do?'

'A reporter called Jane Cooper from the North Yorkshire Moors Group of Newspapers has asked the chief constable if she can accompany a rural beat officer for a full tour of duty. It will entail a whole day's visit, Rhea, to see what we do and how we do it. Your name was one of those put forward and, after due consideration, the chief constable feels your beat is ideal for such a visit.'

'I'm flattered, Sergeant!' I smiled.

'I'd be very worried if I were you,' was his response. 'You'll carry an enormous responsibility that day, Rhea! The reporter will accompany you in your official vehicle throughout your tour of duty, then she will write up the day's events which will appear in all the newspapers of that group. They include the *Ashfordly Gazette*, the *Strensford Post*, the *Harrowby Times*, the *Brantsford Chronicle*, the *Eltering Herald* ... the lot, Rhea. Publicity throughout the whole of our region. And at some stage, a photographer will join you, so you'll have to get your hair cut. Make sure your boots are polished and your trousers are pressed. We want the force to emerge with credit from this exercise. A lot depends on you and don't forget

54

that Ashfordly Section will be under the spotlight! You will be an ambassador for the entire police service, Rhea.'

'I understand, Sergeant; so when do I do this?'

'Next Tuesday. I've changed your duties for that day—you'll perform a ten a.m. to six p.m. tour and will use the Ashfordly Section car. It looks smarter than a Mini-van and I don't think it would be wise to carry a pretty girl reporter on the back of a motor bike. So report here, to Ashfordly Police Station at ten a.m. to collect the car and your passenger. Show Miss Cooper how you spend your working day, Rhea, take her to meet the people, deal with things as they arise, put on a good show and throughout the event never forget you are representing not just Ashfordly Section, but the whole of the North Riding Constabulary—or even the entire nation's police service!'

'I understand, Sergeant,' I assured him once again and almost immediately wondered if I would be given an itinerary for this visit.

That was not the idea behind the scheme, I was sure; the papers wanted to take an honest and unprepared look at the work of a village constable. The truth was that when any operational police officer began a tour of duty he or she had no idea what was going to happen, consequently the preparation of a tightly timed itinerary seemed fraught with danger. The best-laid plans of mice, men and Sergeant Blaketon were likely to go astray and so I gave some thought to my own plans for that day. I favoured showing Miss Cooper a typical day's duty at Aidensfield—but I could only do as I was told.

'You'd better come in early that day,' Blaketon rounded off his instructions. 'You'll have to clean the car before you take it out.'

On the appointed day, therefore, which was a Tuesday in mid-August, I arrived at Ashfordly Police Station at nine o'clock in my old uniform and spent an hour cleaning the car inside and out, then tidied myself and changed into my best outfit to await my guest. Sergeant Blaketon agreed that the station coffee fund could afford a mug of instant coffee for the reporter when she arrived but decided that the station mugs were too chipped and stained to be offered to a visitor. He obtained a smart china cup and saucer from a cupboard in his office—and followed with a matching milk jug and sugar basin. I think in it he kept these items of crockery for visits by the chief constable—normally, he used a mug as battered as ours. The official welcome having been prepared, he asked, 'So what are your plans for the day, Rhea?'

This did surprise me—I had felt sure he would have devised an itinerary but in fact, he was leaving it all to me. I mentally thanked him while wondering if it was really headquarters who had specified the conditions for my role—in other words, the chief constable wanted the reporter to see a rural beat constable doing what he normally did, without any obvious staged incidents or pre-arranged meetings. Who or whatever was behind this plan, I was pleased I was able to make my own arrangements.

I told him I would begin by explaining the structure of the force at section and beat level, using the wall map in the office to illustrate my points. Once we were on the road and touring my beat, I was going to visit a farm to show Miss Cooper how we checked stock registers; I had the renewal of a firearm certificate to deal with which meant inspecting the weapons held by the certificate holder and completing the necessary formalities; I would inspect one of the local pubs at lunchtime to ensure no youngsters were tippling during the school holidays; there was an elderly invalid lady living alone at Thackerston whom I visited when in the area, to see if she needed any help with anything such as shopping or posting letters; I would enter various parish churches on my patch to check that thieves had not raided the offertory boxes or stolen things from the altars; I would introduce her to personalities living on my patch, such as the doctor, the district nurse, special constables, magistrates and others whom we might encounter and would endeavour to deal with anything and anyone requiring immediate attention during our tour.

I had arranged for Mary to provide lunch at our police house in Aidensfield, and explained that the progress of the day really depended upon what happened from an operational point of view. Things like sudden deaths, reported crimes and traffic accidents were always likely to occur, and in some ways, I hoped that an exciting incident did arise.

'Well, you seem to have covered everything. It's a good sample of your routine work. I'm sure you will suitably impress our visitor.'

Jane Cooper arrived at about ten minutes to ten, parking her Triumph Herald in the drive and walking up the path to the front door as we observed her. She was a tall, lithe young woman in her early thirties with long dark hair and a most attractive face and figure.

In a close-fitting, dark-green suit with a rather short skirt, she wore black court shoes and carried a black handbag, hardly a rustic outfit and certainly not one for tramping across fields or splodging through farmyards. I would endeavour to keep her on the cleaner portions of my patch. As she entered the mighty portals of Ashfordly Police Station, Sergeant Blaketon and I were ready and waiting behind the counter.

'I'm from the Yorkshire Moors Group of Newspapers,' she smiled as she came into the general office. 'Jane Cooper.'

'Good morning, Miss Cooper,' beamed Blaketon. 'I am the officer in charge of Ashfordly Section, Sergeant Blaketon is the name,' and he extended his hand for her to shake.

'I'm so pleased you were able to accommodate me. I am the deputy group editor, by the way, so I shall ensure your work is featured in all our titles.'

'We're delighted; it's a real privilege,' beamed Blaketon, clearly quite impressed not only by the woman's good looks and deportment, but by the fact she was no ordinary reporter. A deputy group editor no less!

'And this is your police station, Sergeant? Very compact and well kept, I see,' and she ran her hand across the highly polished brass door knob.

'Yes, we have a good cleaning lady. Now, this is PC Rhea, Nick to his friends. He'll be showing you around his patch today, but let's have coffee first. PC Rhea? If you would, please? We'll take it in my office after I've shown Miss Cooper around the station.'

I noticed Sergeant Blaketon referred to me as PC Rhea when in her presence, not just Rhea. But while he showed Miss Cooper the three cells and tiny outdoor exercise yard, these being the only additional official rooms in the police station apart from his office and the general office, I brewed two mugs of best Ashfordly police station coffee and one smart cupful. We adjourned to his office where he explained the system of supervision from Force Headquarters to Divisional Headquarters, Divisional Headquarters to Sub-Divisional Headquarters, Sub-Divisional Headquarters to Section level (i.e. Ashfordly) and section level to rural beats, i.e. Aidensfield.

Having chatted for about half an hour, he showed her the boundaries of Ashfordly Section and Aidensfield beat, using the wall map in the office, thus stealing part of my proposed routine. Finally, having felt he had made a good impression, he turned to me and said, 'Now, don't forget there will be a photographer around, PC Rhea. Best behaviour and all that ...'

'Ah, yes,' said Jane Cooper. 'I was going to mention that. We're using a freelance; he'll join us later. He's got a job to complete this morning at Malton, so perhaps he can join us sometime during the afternoon?'

'Fine,' I said. 'I've arranged a lunch break at my police house in Aidensfield, for one o'clock. We'll be leaving about quarter to two after we've eaten. He could meet us there, perhaps? Would that be suitable, Miss Cooper?'

'A good idea. Yes, I think that will be fine. Can I use your phone to ring him and suggest that?'

'By all means, Miss Cooper,' beamed Blaketon. I got the impression she could have had anything she wished. Blaketon was clearly impressed by her. And so the arrangements were made. The photographer, Steve Barton, would come to Aidensfield Police House and join us for the earlier part of the second leg of our tour.

'Well, PC Rhea, it's time for your patrol.' Blaketon had no wish to appear lackadaisical in his running of the station and ushered us from the building. 'Do ask PC Rhea about anything at all, Miss Cooper, and if we can help later, when you settle down to write your piece, please call us. I might join you at some stage, and do hope you have an enjoyable and interesting day.'

'I am sure I will. Thank you, Sergeant,' and she dazzled him with one of her lovely smiles. With Sergeant Blaketon having explained the structure of Ashfordly and Aidensfield in relation to the whole force, there was no need for me to repeat the exercise, and so we went straight outside to the waiting car.

'Call me Jane,' she invited as she settled into the passenger seat.

'Thanks, and I'm Nick,' and thus the formalities of Sergeant Blaketon's office were forgotten. Soon we were leaving Ashfordly and heading for the hills in which Aidensfield was situated, with me explaining how the police radio system operated in the car and the sort of incidents which we might expect to be dealt with by that medium. She scribbled in shorthand in a reporter's notebook as we motored along, and I found her to be a charming and interested companion.

We called at a farm and inspected a stock register; we dealt with the renewal of the firearms certificate with me explaining how I had to check the weapons, particularly their serial numbers, and then, as we headed for Crampton church to check the offertory box, a young mother with a little boy at her side flagged us down in the village. The child, called Simon Shaw, aged six, had found a £1 note in the street. I made a record of his find in my official pocket book, told him to keep it for three months, and advised his mother that if it wasn't claimed in that time, it belonged to Simon. His mum was delighted and said it would go into his money box.

As I dealt with these routine matters, I explained the reasons for my actions, particularly the need for me to make a pocket book entry of everything I did. I emphasized the risks involved in handling found money or other objects and explained how some thieves stole wallets or purses, emptied them and threw them away. An innocent person could find them and hand them in to the police, only to be accused of stealing the missing cash. Even the police could be accused of such thefts. So when such items were handed in, the contents were carefully checked in the presence of the finder. It was all good stuff for a reporter—and, of course, I said that some items of found property might be the result of crime, referring to two scouts who discovered a cache of silverware in a ditch. It had been stolen from a country house some months earlier. Such matters, which were routine to a police officer, were of great interest to the general public, I was assured.

Lunchtime came all too quickly and Jane

was delighted to accept Mary's invitation to join us for a meal. In spite of coping with our four children during the school holidays, she had managed to produce a fine piece of roast beef along with Yorkshire pudding and all the accoutrements. It was ready for us prompt at one o'clock as we arrived at the house.

Normally, a police officer was allowed three-quarters of an hour for a meal break during a tour of duty (during which time he or she was still on duty) but on this occasion, I stretched it to an hour. Shortly before two o'clock, the photographer arrived. Steve Barton was a long-haired and rather untidily dressed young man who turned up in a battered Mini car, and he joined us over our cup of tea as we concluded lunch. We'd only just finished our meal when there was a frantic knocking on the front door of the house. The visitor had not chosen to hammer on the office door.

'I'll get it,' said Mary, knowing that some callers did not wish to speak to the constable, but were often salesmen trying to sell an encyclopaedia, gypsies trying to sell pegs, village people selling charity flags or wanting donations, lost salesmen trying to locate farms or business premises, or children coming to play with one or other of our brood.

This arrival, whoever it was, prompted a new line of questioning from Jane; she was anxious to know how the public knew when the village constable was out on duty or off duty, or at home. I told her I was on call twenty-four hours a day and that we did not hoist a flag or flash a blue light from the roof to show when we were in residence!

People called at all hours of the day and night, even during holidays and days off and always expected a swift, polite service. If I was out on patrol, Mary or a 999 call would trace me. But on this occasion I was at home and on duty. Having answered the door, Mary rushed back.

'It's Claude Jeremiah Greengrass!' she said with a look of concern in her eyes. 'And he looks in a bit of a state. He wants you. I've put him in the office.'

'Duty calls!' I said to my visitors, although I must admit I almost groaned aloud upon learning the identity of my visitor. Claude was not the most welcome of callers at this particular time but I knew I must not be so crass in front of a journalist—I had to treat everyone alike without fear or favour. Wondering what the fellow wanted, I hurried into my office which adjoined the house and was closely followed by Jane and the photographer. They were anxious not to miss anything for here was real police work, an unexpected call, an emergency, a drama perhaps—even if it was Claude!

'You'll have to do summat, Constable!' he spoke in evident distress as I entered the office. 'Immediately, if not sooner!'

'Calm down, Claude.' Before my audience, I tried to appear the coolest of constables as I assessed the situation. 'What's the trouble?'

'It's Alfred,' he said. 'He's fallen down a pit shaft on Gelderslack Moor; you'll have to get him out.'

'And you've left him there?' I cried.

'Aye, well, it's full of water, you see, and he's swimming around in circles. He can't climb out, the sides are straight up and down, slippery with it, covered with green moss and slime, but he's keeping afloat. I've nowt in my truck that'll get him out ... you'll need a rope or summat, lifting gear, mebbe, or a crane ...'

'What about the Fire Brigade?' I put to him.

'It'll take ages for them to get there; they're not full-timers round here, you know. Besides, it needs just one extra chap with a rope, so I knew you'd help out.'

'Are you sure that's all that's needed?'

'Aye, 'course I am. Just a helping hand.'

'Right, well, if you think I can do the job,' I began.

'Who is this Alfred?' I heard Jane's voice close to me.

'It's his dog,' I said. 'Alfred. A lurcher ...'

'He's more than just a dog to me!' There was anguish on the old fellow's face now. 'He's my best friend, my companion, my eyes and ears ...'

'He's a poacher's dog,' I informed Jane. 'Not that I'm saying Claude is a poacher, of course, but his dog is very fit and healthy, and he'll not drown. All right Claude. First let me see if I've got the right equipment in the car. A rope you suggest? How deep is this old shaft?'

'Bottomless,' he said. 'Aud Sam from Toft End chucked one of his dead cows down there years ago, and it's not hit the bottom yet! Still going, it is! But

68

it's full of water now, well, very nearly full.'

'So how far down is Alfred?'

'Twenty feet. Ten mebbe. Summat like that.' He could not give me a precise measurement. 'That's why I reckon two chaps with a rope can get him out. We can make a noose for him to swim into as he goes round and round, then hoick him out. That's if he hasn't got dizzy by this time. Can dogs get dizzy, Constable? Swimming in circles for hours on end can't be good for him, can it?'

'If your noose got around his neck, you'd strangle him,' I warned. 'You'll need a loop big enough for him to swim through, so it goes round his shoulders behind his front legs. But yes, you might have a good suggestion. All we need is a good long rope.'

There was a tow rope in the boot of Sergeant Blaketon's car but I felt it was not long enough for the suggested task. 'Joe Scully has a long rope or two at Home Farm,' I recalled. 'For holding weights to keep tarpaulins down on his stacks. I'll see if we can borrow one.'

I rang Joe Scully who had several very long and strong ropes, and when

I explained what it was for, he agreed I could borrow one.

'Right,' I said to Claude. 'You'd better come with me in the car. Jane, can you go with Steve? Follow us—you've got a story!'

'Story?' A look of puzzlement appeared on Claude's grizzly features.

I explained about the presence of Jane and Steve, whereupon Claude's face lit up as he said, 'You mean I'm going to be in the papers? Me and Alfred? We'll be famous, will we?'

'It has all the makings of a very good story about the varied and exciting work of a village policeman,' smiled Jane, and Claude began to warm to the rescue operation. With him in the passenger seat of Sergeant Blaketon's gleaming car, we dropped into Home Farm, collected the rope from Joe and raced out to Gelderslack Moor, a drive of some twenty-five minutes. Steve's gallant little Mini kept pace and soon we were coming to a halt on a track on the slopes below the summit of the moor. The purple heights of the heather-clad slopes rose behind but we were in grassland where the rough road meandered around the side of the dale. I found myself directed by Claude towards a circle of trees in the middle of a moorside field.

'That's it,' Claude pointed out. 'The pit shaft.'

I knew the area. It had once been a busy iron-ore mining district but the boom had ended about a century earlier. Remnants of those industrial days littered Gelderslack Dale, and this old pit shaft was one of them. Situated in the middle of a field, it looked like a small copse of mature hawthorns surrounded by a wooden fence, but in fact it was a very deep pit shaft. Claude opened the gate of the field and we drove in, parking as close as possible to the shaft.

It was at that point that the radio of the car burbled into life and I heard Sergeant Blaketon's voice calling me from Ashfordly police station.

'Location, please, Delta Alpha Four Seven,' he asked.

'Old pit shaft, Low Hag Farm fields near Gelderslack Moor,' I told him.

'Is there an incident, Rhea?' was his next question.

'A minor one, Sergeant,' I assured him. 'A dog trapped in a pit shaft. Rescue operation in hand.'

'A nice one for the Press! I will rendezvous with you, Rhea,' he said. 'I'll come as soon as I can.'

'Message received and understood,' I responded. 'Four Seven out.' Then turning to my guests, I said, 'Sergeant Blaketon's coming to pay me an official visit so I think we should get this job done before he gets here.'

'I couldn't agree more!' And the thought of his old adversary arriving to witness the distress of Alfred prompted Claude to press me into speedier action. With Claude rushing as fast as he could, his old army greatcoat flapping at his heels, I followed him to the fence and looked inside the ring of trees. It was a circular pit about twelve feet in diameter and it looked rather like a small pond surrounded by densely growing hawthorns. This was deceptive, but the presence of the stone lining told us it was a man-made shaft of great but immeasurable depth. The first thing I had noticed was the appalling stench which rose from the surface of the stirred-up water. This water had not been disturbed for generations and I did not even attempt to guess what had flowed into it from the farm and fields nearby. There was a distinct aroma of cowhouses about the place. And there, in the oily and litter-encrusted water, was the dirty grey figure of Alfred the lurcher. He was still swimming around in a large circle and carried a rusty tin in his mouth. He was snorting through his nose as he insisted on carrying the tin, his legs paddling for all they were worth beneath the surface.

But I could see the problem—the stone lining of the old pit was perpendicular and covered with green moss and slime. The dog could not climb out that way and no one could climb down those walls without an aid of some kind, although I did note that some stout branches of the hawthorns did overhang the water. I thought they might bear the weight of an adult person; someone in that water might be able to haul themselves out by utilizing those branches, providing the parent tree was sufficiently well rooted. But dogs didn't behave like that. Alfred just swam round and round as we watched, his eyes on his master who was calling his name. I reckoned the distance from the top of the shaft down to Alfred was about ten feet as Claude had intimated. But it did present a problem.

'How on earth did he get in there?' was

the obvious question.

I asked this as I tried to work out the most suitable means of effecting a rescue and must admit that I had now forgotten about the ever-present reporter and photographer.

'It was this hare.' Claude started to blink as he began his explanation. 'It was running across this field, and, well, you know how hares twist and turn when they're being chased. Well, this 'un galloped towards this pit shaft with Alfred going flat out after him and at the last minute the hare turned away. They do that, you know. Trouble was, Alfred didn't turn. He kept going straight on, he couldn't pull up, you see, he was galloping that fast, and he shot straight through that gap in the fence.' Claude pointed to a broken spar in the railings. 'Well, he'd have no idea what was behind there, would he? A pit full of stinking water. Next thing I knew there was this almighty splash and he was in that mucky water ... it stank summat awful, Mr Rhea, after he disturbed the muck on the surface, stirred it up right rotten. Stank like a midden, it did, with a few rotten eggs and cow pats mixed in. Worse than a gorilla's armpit, I can tell you. Anyroad, he started to swim around like he is now ... and I couldn't get him out. He'll swim for hours yet, he's a fit lad, Mr Rhea, but he can't go on for ever. Well, I mean, what could I do? I went for help and was passing your house when I thought of you, you see, I thought you might help me.'

I could see that he was genuinely distressed and as I was pondering the most suitable method of attempting a rescue, Steve Barton was already taking photographs of the scenario, including the swimming Alfred and his tin. After a short debate, it seemed the most simple solution would be to create a loop at the end of the rope, along with a knot which would permit the loop to be tightened. The loop could then be lowered into the water and if Alfred could be persuaded to swim through it so that it was around his shoulders and behind his front legs, we could haul rapidly upon it and drag him up the side of the pit. Relying on the knowledge of knots I had gained in the Boy Scouts, I fashioned a large loop, secured by a round turn and two half hitches, at the end of our rope. The round turn and two half hitches would enable the noose to be tightened when required. Reaching out as far as I dare over the reeking water, I lowered the loop as Claude tried to coax Alfred to swim into it but the rope floated on the top.

There was so much floating rubbish that the rope could not sink (it would probably have floated on the top anyway) and thus the dog could not swim through the loop. Alfred's brisk front leg action simply swept the loop aside as he ploughed relentlessly onwards. We thought about lashing a brick to the loop so that it would sink sufficiently for the dog to swim through it, but decided the weight would cause the loop to close up. Try as we might, we could not sink the rope into the effluvium in a way that enabled Alfred to swim into our carefully crafted loop, so I came up with another idea.

'If I climb along one of those branches,' —I indicated the most sturdy of the hawthorns—'I could hold the rope in a huge loop, as wide as my arms. If we weighted it at the bottom to make two corners from it, they would sink into the water as deep as necessary and I'm sure we could persuade Alfred to swim into it. I could then tighten the rope around his

76

body and all of us could haul him out.'

With a twig, I drew a picture in the dust on the ground and Claude saw my logic. 'Are you sure that branch'll bear your weight?' he expressed some concern at my plan. 'Mebbe I should try it? It is my dog.'

'I'm younger than you, Claude,' I heard myself say. 'More agile too, I'd guess. If I fasten myself to the rope, with one end tied to the back axle of the car, I could be hauled out myself, if I fall in. And I can swim!'

And so the plan was put into operation. Placing my uniform cap on the ground, I climbed over the fence rather gingerly and stood on the rim of the pit, testing the strength of the thick hawthorn branch with my foot.

It did not give; it seemed to be quite safe, and the tree's large trunk emerged from the earth beneath the fence. That tree had been there for years; it was surely as safe as anything could be. We drew Blaketon's car as close as possible to the fence and I lashed one end of the rope around the back axle, using a fisherman's knot. Then, with the other end, I made a massive loop and found a couple of small stones which I lashed to the rope with bits of string from Claude's pocket. If I lifted the rope with each of my hands spread to their full width, it formed a square with the stones at the bottom. This was my dog-saver; I tested the movement of the round turn and two half hitches and found it did slide quite freely. I hoped the dampness would not frustrate my sliding knot. Thus, if I went out on to the branch, lowered my square loop into the water as far as possible and persuaded Alfred to swim into it, I could pull on the rope and hopefully catch him. If things worked as I hoped, the noose would tighten and Alfred could be lifted out.

Like so many schemes of similar doubtful practicality, the only way this could be tested was to put it into action. If I fell into the water, the rope would be my salvation. I had forgotten about the cameraman clicking away as I tested the security of the rope's attachment to the car and ventured out on to the limb of the tree. I bounced up and down upon it once or twice, clutching the rope in case it snapped, but it was quite solid. Scratching my face with the spikes of the hawthorn,

I inched outwards, moving steadily further and further above the malodorous surface of the water as Alfred continued to swim beneath me, now watching me with some interest.

So far so good.

My confidence was now increasing as I found myself directly above Alfred's circular marathon swimming route. I stood upright and prepared the rope, extending my arms so that my proposed loop would be as wide as my reach. I held a part in each hand, then lowered my large loop gradually into the water. The stones helped the rope to sink until it was about two feet below the surface, enough to accommodate Alfred's paddling paws. Thus I had formed a rough kind of square, a frame of rope for Alfred to swim into. And he did. As his front paddling paws crossed the rope beneath the water, Claude slowed his progress with a call of his name, and at that instant, I hauled on the rope. I was delighted when it slipped behind his front legs and then the knot began to slide along the rope, tightening rapidly ... Alfred began to struggle as he felt the rope beneath him, but he was too late to escape. The rope was in position around his belly and shoulders, neatly behind his front legs. I'd got him! He'd not be strangled as we hauled him from the pit.

With surprising ease, I found the rope tightened around his thin body but he began to thrash about in the water, sending up a suffocating pong as he stirred up yet more of that rancid surface. But he could not escape. We'd caught him so that he could be made free. He was still in the water, however; the next task would be to lift him out.

And that's when the problems started. As I took his weight upon the rope, there was an ominous crack and the tip of the hawthorn branch suddenly sank; it had fractured close to the trunk of the tree. The extra weight of the wet dog had been enough to break it.

It did not snap completely off, but fractured sufficiently for the part upon which I was standing to dip towards the water. And I fell headlong off it, right into the mess below.

It is difficult to recall precisely what happened next but I did have the presence of mind to hang on to the rope; suddenly, I was thrashing about among a foul-smelling mess with Alfred doing likewise near my head to the shouts of alarm and encouragement from the audience at the rim of the pit. Happily, the rope was secured to the back axle of Blaketon's car and instinctively, I knew that if I could hang on I could clamber up the rope to safety. At this stage, I had no idea whether or not the dog was still within the loop I had so carefully prepared for him, but after I allowed myself to calm down and spit out the foul-tasting and evil-smelling brew which had gone into my mouth, I began to haul on the rope. I found myself moving through the mess towards the wall of the pit, hauling myself forward hand over hand; the broken branch of the hawthorn was above me and I was able to seize it with my other hand. Still anchored to the tree but moving at my touch, I managed to utilize the branch to drag myself close to the wall. In spite of the slipperiness of the moss and grime which covered the stones, there were small crevices which formed toe-holds.

And so, hauling on the rope now with both hands and using my feet in what toe-holds I could find, I slowly climbed up until Claude Jeremiah Greengrass, Steve and Jane helped me over the rim, panting, exhausted and reeking of unimaginably bad smells.

As I lay for a few moments to gather my breath and to breathe in the beautiful fresh moorland air, I heard sounds below, whimpering and whining, and realized that Alfred was now being dragged from the depths by Claude. The rope was hurting him, but he could not free himself as he was hauled to the surface. And all of this was being photographed by Steve Barton and reported by Jane Cooper. As the dog was brought to the rim, I got to my feet, with gallons of foul water pouring out of my uniform. I was thoroughly soaked and completely smothered in the most evil-smelling effluvium—and so was Alfred.

'Mr Rhea,'—there were tears in Claude's eyes—'I don't know how to thank you, honest I don't ... I mean, that took courage ...'

'Forget it, Claude,' I said. 'I know you'd do the same for me. Now, let's get home, I want to get cleaned up!'

'And I might give Alfred a bath, he does stink, doesn't he?'

'He does, rather,' and I uttered the understatement of the year.

At this stage, Alfred shook himself

vigorously so that a fine spray of the gunge enveloped us all, most of it landing on my cap which I had thoughtfully discarded.

'That was wonderful, Nick,' beamed Jane. 'Really, we couldn't have asked for anything better. Steve's got some wonderful pictures.'

'Smashing,' chuckled the photographer. 'You and that dog down there ... brilliant.'

'Well, if you can bear with me while I go home and get changed, we can continue,' I advised them.

'There's no need, not on our behalf,' said Jane. 'I've got enough here for a wonderful feature. Steve and I will leave you now; we can get to work on the feature and you'll need to get cleaned and put your feet up ...'

I didn't say that my day's duty was not yet over. It was only 3.30 and I had a further two and a half hours of patrolling to complete before ending my shift, but I realized I could not hope to provide them with another story like this one. Jane got a quote from Claude, praising the constabulary for saving his best friend from a smelly death, and they left in Steve's Mini car, saying they'd collect Jane's Triumph Herald from Ashfordly

Police Station *en route*.

As they left, Claude shouted, 'Come on, Constable, my dog's starting to shiver after that cold bath,' and he hurried over to Blaketon's car. Before I could stop him, he'd opened the passenger door, calling to Alfred, 'In you get, son!'

Alfred leapt on to the passenger seat, dripping filth all over, then leapt into the rear, shook himself again and lay down; there was putrescent smelling muck and water everywhere and when I joined them, I added to the general abomination which was now Sergeant Blaketon's car. Claude Jeremiah was the cleanest and purest-scented living thing in that car at that moment, something I suspect Sergeant Blaketon would never believe. But I had no choice about the use of the car—it was the only way to get home for my bath.

Then as I started to drive away from the pit shaft, Sergeant Blaketon arrived in my Mini-van, smart and proud, anxious to see what I had been doing and wondering how I was coping with the Press. He pulled up just inside the field.

'All finished, is it?' he asked, climbing out. 'I saw them going down the lane. Nice girl, that editor.'

'Trust you to get here when it's all over!' grinned Claude Jeremiah Greengrass from the passenger seat. 'That's not the way to get your name in the papers. Sergeant Blaketon.'

'What are you doing here, Greengrass? Has he been arrested, Rhea? If not, why not?'

I got out of the car to address him but before I could explain things, he cried, 'My God, Rhea, what's this? You're soaked ... and that foul smell ... Greengrass! Is it your socks? Or is it just you! I'd recognize that smell anywhere! Rhea, what in the name of the great god Beelzebub has been going on? Is that Greengrass's dog, in my car? Messing up my clean leather. God, the stench is dreadful ...'

'Well, Sergeant, it's like this ...'

'And just look at that mess!' He went closer to peer into his once-pristine vehicle, then held his nose as his eyes began to water. 'God Almighty, Rhea! Have you been carrying manure in my car? It's like a muck cart in there. You'll clean that leather until it shines, Rhea, you understand? Shines, without any trace of a smell. And I never thought I would see the day when Greengrass and his dog, and a pitshaft full of excrement and farmyard manure, were in my car, all at the same time ... that's all I need ...'

'Sorry, Sergeant, but it was like this ...' I tried again.

'Did that reporter witness this fiasco?' was his next question.

I could see the frown of absolute dismay beginning to appear on his face.

'Yes, she did, and she got an interview with Claude.'

'And that photographer? Did he picture all this?'

I nodded.

'And did you say she interviewed Greengrass? She actually got close enough to that smelly heap of humanity to talk to him? Why would anyone want to interview him, Rhea? Tell me that!'

'This constable saved my dog's life, I'll have you know.' Claude was now out of the car and beaming at Blaketon. 'He deserves a big pat on the back, a medal even, not a bollocking from you! You wait till you see the papers, Blaketon, and all them photographs, then you'll know what it's like to dive into a stinking pit of slime to rescue a dog as loving and faithful as my Alfred.'

'If you'd told me it was Greengrass's dog you were going to rescue, I'd have told you not to bother ... So what happened to you, Rhea?'

'I fell in,' I started to explain.

'Fell in? And who rescued you? Greengrass?'

'Well, yes, as a matter of fact. He helped to get me out.'

'And you mean to tell me those journalists witnessed one of my constables being rescued by that man Greengrass, and they got pictures of that as well?'

'Well, I suppose so, Sergeant ...'

'I can't trust you to do a proper job, can I, Rhea?' I had the distinct impression he was not very pleased with the outcome of my actions. 'I should have given this job to Ventress. Right, go home and get cleaned up, clean my car as best you can, then come down to my office in a fresh-smelling uniform. I want a full explanation and a written report about this fiasco, every bit of it!'

'Yes, Sergeant,' I said meekly.

Fortunately, the article, when it appeared a week later, was highly complimentary and made my efforts appear to be far more glamorous and daring than they really were.

The photograph of the rescue depicted me in the water clutching the rope with one hand and Alfred with the other, and the article did embrace the other aspects of my work. As a result, I got several letters of appreciation from animal charities, plus one from the chief constable and a crate of beer from Claude Jeremiah Greengrass.

Later, a typed order signed by Sergeant Blaketon was placed on the internal noticeboard. It said, 'Under no circumstances will dirty dogs be allowed to travel in police vehicles based at Ashfordly Police Station.'

I refrained from making any comment about that.

There was another curious manifestation of the Press reportage in Ashfordly, one which caused the constables of that police station to chuckle to themselves at the expense of Sergeant Blaketon. It came in the form of a district correspondent's supposedly secret adoration of our sergeant.

There is little doubt the lady in question had a gargantuan crush on our worthy leader, a crush that could be likened to a teenager's hero worship. She was called Mildred Levington. Her husband was a retired solicitor and they lived in a neat bungalow on the edge of Ashfordly where Mr Levington's retirement enabled him to spend more time growing prize chrysanthemums and organizing flower shows.

Mildred, who had worked as a clerk for a timber yard, had also retired but she lacked her husband's enthusiasm for flowers and flower shows. I suspect she felt that Hubert might spend more time with her in retirement, visiting places, eating out and exploring the countryside of Britain. But he didn't; he neglected her in favour of his floral passions. Alone for much of the time and in her early sixties, Mildred was anxious to make her retirement years as useful and as interesting as possible; she wanted to fruitfully occupy her ample spare time whilst, ideally, meeting interesting people and getting involved with the life of the town.

The answer to her desires came in the form of an advertisement in the *Ashfordly Gazette*. It announced the paper was seeking a district correspondent and after studying the requirements of the job, Mildred considered it an excellent means of getting involved with community matters and at the same time earning a few pounds.

In simple terms, her role would be to look out for and then report very local news. It supplemented the work of the resident professional reporters and entailed coverage of events like Mr Levington's flower shows along with whist drives, funerals, parish council meetings, infant school sports days and a whole range of other local meetings, functions and occurrences.

Mildred applied for the post and was successful; she would be paid a few pence per line of published news and the deadline was 10 a.m. each Wednesday morning. In time, it seemed that most of Mildred's work would consist of the accurate reproduction of elongated lists of names of people who had won boxes of chocolates, rosettes or bottles of sherry or cheap wine in raffles or at tombola, or who were mourners at funerals.

But she did get around the town, she did meet people and she did get invited to all kinds of functions, chiefly so that the organizers would get their names in the paper. As a consequence, she typed long lists of names of people who had won raffles or attended funerals and these were published in the weekly 'Local News' columns. If this was hardly the stuff of national newspaper headlines, there was a serious and very sound financial purpose behind those never-ending lists of names. Apart from earning Mildred some lineage money, the fact that a person's name appeared in the newspaper meant that person would rush out and buy a copy. It was an ideal way of increasing sales. This, therefore, was Mildred's new job and there is no doubt that sales of the *Gazette* soared in Ashfordly thanks to her listing of many names.

In time, though, we began to notice a certain flavour to her reports. It is perhaps prudent at this stage to describe Mildred. A tall, very slim and rather plain woman with a reddish face that never smiled, she had grey hair permed in the style of the 1940s and wore thick stockings, flat-heeled brown shoes with buckles and cheap frocks which concealed any semblance of a figure she might have had. Plain was a word often used to describe her.

A pair of round spectacles graced a face which had never seen make-up in its life and her only adornment was a necklace in the form of a thin gold-coloured chain bearing a locket. None of us had any idea of the contents of that locket. No ear-rings, lipstick or other adornment ever came her way and it was difficult to imagine her ever being a young woman or a girl. I doubt if true romance or passion had ever stirred her emotions in spite of her courtship and marriage to Hubert. It seemed the sole object of his passion was flowers.

The absence of heart-pounding desire in her marriage could explain her fixation with Sergeant Blaketon. His manly figure, stern voice, powers of command and decisive leadership, position of authority within the town and, of course, his extremely smart uniform, had apparently combined to produce within her love-starved breast, the rapidly beating heart of someone very much in love. It must be said that she never openly declared or revealed that love—not that she ever would, of course, being a respectable married woman of some standing in Ashfordly. But even married ladies like Mildred Levington can adore champions and may possess submerged urges and desires even if conventions conspire to prevent them from openly declaring such love.

It was Sergeant Blaketon's talk to Ashfordly Womens' Institute which pro-vided me with the first hint of Mildred's devotion. Entitled 'Policing in the 1960s', he had spoken to a group meeting of several Women's Institutes at Ashfordly Town Hall, and Mildred had reported the event. Her account of his participation read,

Sergeant Oscar Blaketon, the smartly dressed officer in sole charge of Ashfordly Police Station, delivered a superb exposition of the heavy responsibilities of policing the community in a rapidly changing social climate. Speaking without notes and making full use of an impressive vocabulary of words, Sergeant Blaketon enthralled those present with his smartness, authoritative manner, ready wit, deep knowledge and his clear commitment to public service. It was a superbly crafted and well-delivered talk which was enjoyed by all.

I was in Ashfordly Police Station the morning this report appeared in print. PC Alf Ventress was reading the paper as Sergeant Blaketon walked into the office, and he said, 'By Jove, Sarge, you've an admirer here!'

'What are you talking about, Ventress?'

Blaketon was not in a particularly good mood that morning.

'That talk of yours last week, to the WI,' grinned Ventress. 'It sounds as though you were a hit!'

Blaketon took the paper from Alf and read the report, blushing slightly as he said, 'It's a perfectly factual report, Ventress. They did enjoy what I told them. I am a capable public speaker, you know. I know how to dress, I know how important it is to be smart when in uniform and particularly when representing the Constabulary before a critical audience. And I do get my points across.'

It was the following day when Mildred appeared at the counter of the police station; I was manning the telephone while Alf Ventress was attending Eltering Court as a witness in a case of a lorry driver having no driving licence.

'Hello, Mrs Levington,' I greeted her.

'Is Sergeant Blaketon in?' she asked, and, recalling Alf's earlier comments, I detected the faint hint of a blush on her cheeks. Under normal circumstances, I would probably have not noticed her high colour or the hint of excitement in her demeanour.

'Yes, can I ask what the matter is?'

'Yes, Constable. I am the *Gazette's* district correspondent for Ashfordly and I wondered if I might pop in regularly to see if there is anything to report, from a police point of view. I asked for the sergeant because I thought Sergeant Blaketon in person might have to give permission for matters to be released to the Press.'

'Yes, that's true, so you'd better speak to him about it. I'll get him,' I promised her, and went into his office. When I told him the nature of her enquiry, he sighed and said, 'I'll talk to her.'

'Good morning, Mrs Levington.' He managed to produce a wide smile for her as he entered the enquiry office and I could see that her blush and excitement had intensified. 'What can I do for you?'

She repeated her request and he pursed his lips as if pondering the matter in great depth and said, 'Yes, I am sure there are matters over which we could usefully co-operate. Non-policy matters, for example, non-confidential matters, matters of great public interest to the people of this locality. Now, PC Ventress did rescue a kitten from a sack in the river a couple of months ago but that is old news ... but that is precisely the sort of thing that might interest you, I believe?'

'Oh, yes, that would be wonderful, Sergeant. Bravery especially by yourself, good deeds done, crime prevention advice as you said in your excellent talk to the WI meeting, campaigns against litter or speeding, police involvement with community matters. There is a never-ending range of potential newsworthy items.'

He interrupted her effusive flow and he said, 'Well, yes, I am sure we can find something for you on a regular basis. Rhea, you've seen the occurrence book this morning? Is there anything recent that might provide material for Mrs Levington?'

'There were those lost drugs, Sergeant. That lady who'd got something from her doctor for her heart ... little red pills in a box ... she lost them in town yesterday and we were worried in case children found them and thought they were sweets.'

'Absolutely right, Rhea. Right. We can't reveal the name of the loser, Mrs Levington, but there were a hundred red pills in a small white cardboard box. It's got "Ashfordly Medical Practice" on the label, with the name of the pills and the patient. It was lost somewhere in Ashfordly town centre between eleven a.m. and three p.m. yesterday. The finder should bring them here and we will return them to the loser. Maybe you could put that in the paper, stressing the danger to children?'

'Yes, of course. This is ideal, Sergeant. May I call regularly?'

'By all means,' he oozed, and off she went.

When the report appeared, it began,

Sergeant Oscar Blaketon, the officer in charge of Ashfordly Police Station, warned the public to beware of a hundred red pills in a small white box which were lost in the town this week. If found, they should be returned to the sergeant in person. With the professional assurance and style of one who is accustomed to taking instant command in highly dangerous situations, Sergeant Blaketon warned the public, 'Children are especially at risk if they swallow these tablets thinking they are sweets'.

'She's done it again!' beamed Alf Ventress when he read that report.

Mildred repeated her glorification of

Blaketon in the following weeks, with reports like,

After a spaniel was run over and killed by a lorry in Ashfordly on Thursday, the charismatic leader of the town's police, Sergeant Oscar Blaketon, speaking movingly with deep emotion in his voice, said, 'The death of an animal in such circumstances is always a tragedy, but dog owners are advised to keep them on leads when in the vicinity of moving traffic'.

Another report said,

Following a concert in Ashfordly Town Hall by Brantsford Brass Band, the peace-keeping leader of the town's police, Sergeant Oscar Blaketon, said, 'The presence of my officers certainly prevented an outbreak of violence by would-be hooligans. It is not very funny having a carrot thrust up your trumpet in the middle of a scherzo'.

The report concluded:

It is thanks to officers of the calibre of Sergeant Blaketon that our town is able to enjoy peace and tranquillity in these troubled times.

I liked one of her reports which read,

The generosity and philanthropic nature of our police service was exemplified when Sergeant Oscar Blaketon, the genial senior officer at Ashfordly Police Station, handed back the first prize of a cuckoo clock which he won in a raffle for the Red Cross. The prize was then won by Mrs Latimer of Elm Close who does not have a cuckoo clock, and she said, 'I really do think our police are wonderful. If you get the time, thank a policeman'.

As the reports increased in number to further the admiration of our esteemed sergeant, Alf Ventress would cut them out and pin them on the police station noticeboard, taking care to do so when Blaketon was on leave or enjoying a day off. Over the weeks, we enjoyed a wonderful selection—*Sergeant Blaketon, the courteous leader of Ashfordly Police, said the force had no objection to a procession of Girl Guides being routed through the market place.*

Or, *The speaker and prize-giver at the Ashfordly Cricket Club annual dinner will be Sergeant Oscar Blaketon, a fine sportsman, umpire and renowned after-dinner speaker.*

And, *A campaign for clear signs to indicate*

the location of the public toilets in Ashfordly was given a boost by Sergeant Oscar Blaketon, the highly respected commander of the local police force. He said, 'One of our most regular questions is about the location of the public toilets. Much valuable time could be saved if the toilets were clearly signed and our officers could then concentrate on more important duties'.

The judge at next week's Horticultural Society's annual show in the town hall will be Sergeant Oscar Blaketon of Ashfordly Constabulary, a man known for his sensitive appreciation of flowers and things of great beauty. Few local people know more about vegetables, especially marrows, and his judgements are eagerly awaited. He will also judge a special competition—a garden in a tea cup.

At the August meeting of Elsinby WI, the guest speaker was Sergeant Oscar Blaketon, the stylish leader of Ashfordly Police who spoke beautifully with immense sincerity about 'Policing in a rural community' and afterwards revealed a tremendous artistic flair when he judged the best-decorated spoon competition. The winner was Mrs Victoria Price, of whom the sergeant said, 'I've never seen a more unusual dipper'.

A procession of persons involved in service to the public will walk from Ashfordly market-place to the parish church next Sunday. A joint service based on the theme 'Peace and Service' will follow at 3 p.m. Among the participants will be members of the Fire Service, Ambulance Service, post office, telephonists, British Rail, doctors, nurses, dentists, veterinary surgeons, county and district council officials, road men, dustbin men and others. Leading the walk will be Sergeant Oscar Blaketon, the officer in charge of Ashfordly Police, who will be resplendent in his uniform and representing the North Riding Constabulary. The warm-hearted sergeant is regarded as the ideal symbol of the 'public service' theme of the gathering.

It was obvious that the purpose of this kind of reporting would eventually make itself clear to Sergeant Blaketon, more so because some of the residents of Ashfordly began to tease him. Many were the husbands of lady members of various organizations who had heard Mildred speak to them in glowing terms about the behaviour and appeal of the

101

smart sergeant; the ladies knew she was in awe of the fellow, that he was her dashing hero, a masterly man, dark, mysterious and handsome ... The ladies had spoken to their husbands about it, and they in turn had made fun of Blaketon—to his face. Blaketon had also come into the police station one day when he was off duty and found one of the cuttings on the noticeboard.

It meant, in short, that Mildred's devotion would have to be brought to an end; Blaketon would have to do something about Mildred's style of reporting. His first action was to ring the editor of the *Ashfordly Gazette*. I was in the office when he made the call and could hear his side of the conversation.

After making contact with the editor, he said, 'I'd like you to edit her reports, Mr Marshall, just to eliminate the unnecessary stuff ... the silly woman's making a mockery of me. I can assure you I am not encouraging her in any way.'

There was a pause, after which he said, 'What do you mean? You already cut out the really juicy bits? And everybody in the office can't wait to see what she's written?'

And he finished with, 'Well, I must have words with her myself then. I can't have this kind of stuff appearing in my local paper and I don't care if she does worship the ground I walk on.'

There was a long pause and then he came into the general office where I was checking the register of licensed premises.

'Rhea,' he said, 'I am exasperated. That bloody woman is making my life a misery. The editor says she sends in all kinds of mush to him and he cuts most of it out. It gives his office staff a laugh and they can't wait to see what Mildred's written about me, so he leaves the tame bits in to please her, to encourage her to send in more reports ... it seems her reports do sell papers, Rhea. I can imagine it! All the folk in this town are buying the paper to try and work out what's going on between me and that woman ... it's not as if she's attractive, damn it. What can I do, Rhea?'

'Find another woman, Sergeant!' I grinned.

'I've got one,' he muttered. 'One's enough for any feller. But Mrs Blaketon doesn't like appearing at public events. She's not a joiner, as you know, she never presents prizes or makes speeches.'

'No, what I meant was that you should show a very keen interest in another woman when Mildred's around to witness it.'

'I'd have my wife down on me like a ton of bricks if I showed undue interest in somebody else ...'

'Then tell her what's happening and get her approval for whatever action you take.'

He wandered back into his office to think things over but did not mention the matter for a long time. Eventually, however, I did notice a change in Mildred's style of reporting. It happened after Sergeant Blaketon had been asked to address the annual general meeting of Ashfordly Town Council in the town hall. His brief was to highlight changes in the method of rural policing so that councillors would be up-to-date with any possible changes. Mildred had been present to report the event and when it appeared in the *Gazette*, it simply said, *The meeting was addressed by Sergeant O. Blaketon.*

The following week, a report said, *At the annual dinner of Ashfordly Snooker League, Sergeant O. Blaketon presented the Wallace Trophy to Mr Sidney Burton as winner of the individual championship for the fifth successive year.* And another item said, *The Ashfordly Lorry Driver of the Year Award was presented to Keith Dent of Dent Cattle Transporters by Sergeant O. Blaketon of Ashfordly Police.*

There were no instances of glorification and it seemed there had been a cooling-off by Mildred so far as her one-sided romance with Sergeant Blaketon was concerned. Furthermore, whenever she called at the police station, she was quite happy to talk to any of the constables in her pursuit of news items. No longer did she seek personal interviews or comments from the object of her secret passion. Quite suddenly, therefore, the wonderful language of her Blaketon reports was eliminated and in some ways, I was sorry. Her reports were so entertaining.

'How did you do it, Sergeant?' I asked him quietly some time later.

'My wife's youngest sister came to stay with us for a couple of weeks,' he smiled. 'She's a very attractive woman, Rhea, so whenever I had an official engagement, I took her along and made a great show of fussing over her. Mildred knew it wasn't Mrs Blaketon and took the huff ... I know Mildred dislikes men who flirt with ladies who are not their wives and who commit adultery.'

And so the deed was done. But within a month, Mildred's reports were glowing again, this time in favour of Rudolph Burley, the Aidensfield auctioneer—it began with a report that *the ruggedly good-looking Rudolph Burley presented the awards at the annual meeting of the Ashfordly Cat Club ...*

I would wait and see how things developed before I decided whether or not to ask Sergeant Blaketon to give Rudolph some advice based on his experience in dealing with amorous and hero-worshipping local correspondents.

3 Missing From Home

An old man's wit may wander
ere he die.
Alfred, Lord Tennyson (1809-1892)

During a conversation with the Aidensfield district nurse, Margot Horsefield, she mentioned the quote at the head of this chapter but eliminated any reference to the word *wit*. She was trying to tell me that an old man—any old man—rather than just the wit or mind of the fellow, might wander before he died. Old ladies were also liable to do this, she affirmed. And she was right. Within a very short time, I had two examples involving old gentlemen and they were followed by another involving an old lady. The tale of Edna Waggett is dealt with later in this book.

Nurse Margot Horsefield was a dark-haired and eminently sensible woman in her mid-thirties whose husband owned and ran a greengrocer's shop in Ashfordly. Both lived in Aidensfield, however, where they had a beautiful stone cottage which overlooked the war memorial. They busied themselves with life in the village and had more spare time than most, chiefly because they had no children. Whether this was by design or otherwise was never known because neither talked about it but there is little doubt she was a splendid and popular nurse, ideal for such an isolated rural community. Her work and mine occasionally overlapped and we would regularly meet in the course of our respective perambulations around the district.

If I had cause to worry about someone living alone, for example, or if I came across children and women with suspicious bruises or found anything which I felt required some discreet medical attention, then I would notify Margot. I knew she would respond with the utmost discretion and professional competence. In return, she kept me informed of matters which she felt came within the scope of my work and the case of old Mr Chesterfield was one example. In this instance, I had emerged from the post office just as she was drawing to a halt outside in her little green Morris. She climbed out, smoothed the skirt of her blue uniform and waved, indicating she wished to speak to me.

'Morning, Nick,' she greeted as I approached. 'Just the man I was hoping to see!'

'Not trouble, I hope!' was my fairly predictable reply.

'And I hope not too!' she grinned. 'It's about old Mr Chesterfield. Alan's father. You've come across him?'

'Alan's dad? No, I can't say I've met him.' I frowned as I tried to recollect the man she was speaking about. 'Does he live locally?'

'He does now,' she said. 'He moved here from Scarborough, he's come back to live with his son, Alan and Alan's wife. You'll know them, they're at High Newbiggin Farm.'

'Yes, I know Alan and Jenny very well,' I told her. 'Nice people.'

'Right, well, Alan's mother died two or three years ago and his dad managed to look after himself for a while afterwards. He did quite well even though he missed his wife, but then his mind began to deteriorate. He took to wandering away from the old folks' bungalow where he lived. That was at Scarborough.'

'I remember Alan once saying his dad lived at Scarborough,' I recalled.

'He was very happy there. In fact, both Mr and Mrs Chesterfield liked Scarborough. When they were still working on the farm at Aidensfield, they always went to Scarborough for their occasional days out, it was almost like a holiday for them, and so when they retired they decided to settle there. Anyway, after Mrs Chesterfield died, poor old Vincent got a bit lonely and started wandering away from his house. Scarborough police had a few alerts to look out for him and they always found him, usually on the foreshore gazing out to sea. The old chap always maintained he was just having a nice walk and that he'd find his own way home. He always said he wasn't lost, claiming he knew where he was. Anyway, from Alan's point of view, the worry was too much, especially due to the distance from his father, so recently he brought his dad back to Aidensfield to live on the farm. It's a big place with plenty of room, and the old fellow has his own rooms—lounge, kitchen and bedroom. It's ideal—he can look after himself and be alone if necessary, but the family's always on hand if there's a problem.'

'I've no doubt I'll come across him when I pay them a visit,' I said.

'His name is Vincent,' she reminded me. 'Vincent Chesterfield. In his prime, he was a fine man, Nick, a proud man and highly respected. He was well known hereabouts and some of his contemporaries are still around. He's met up with some of them and likes nothing better than a good natter over a pint of bitter. He was a farmer at High Newbiggin before he retired about twelve years ago. When he left the farm, Alan, being the only child, took over. So the place is still in the family.'

'All that happened before I was posted to Aidensfield,' I realized. 'So, why are you telling me about old Mr Chesterfield?'

'As I said, in recent months, he became prone to wandering away from his home in Scarborough and that means he might still be liable to go wandering even while he's living at the farm. I know his family is nearby so they're able to keep an eye on him and it helps that the farm is a long way off the beaten track, but there are still plenty of places for him to go astray. If he wandered on to the moors in winter or bad weather, well, he could die as you know. So, Nick, I thought you ought to be told that he's in the district and is a potential problem. One of these days, you might come across him in the village or on the moors. If you do, and if he looks lost, you'll know where he's come from!'

'And I shall return him safe and sound to the bosom of his family,' I smiled. 'So what's he look like?'

She described him as a man of medium height with a rather stocky build who was in his late seventies. He had a round, cheerful face, blue eyes, horn-rimmed spectacles, a good head of thick white hair and a slight hearing difficulty.

He usually wore a grey flat cap, grey flannel trousers, a hacking jacket with a grey background colour and black brogue shoes; he was quite well dressed, his clothes were not shabby or cheap and he was fairly spritely for his age. He used a walking stick and did like walking briskly over quite long distances—he could walk four or five miles without any great difficulty and his general appearance was one of a man in total possession of his faculties. Sadly, though, he was *not* in total possession of those faculties—his mind did cause problems from time to time and he sometimes forgot who he was and where he lived.

I thanked Margot for this information and made a mental note of the old man's physical appearance in the certain knowledge that I would encounter him in the fairly near future.

In the weeks that followed, I did notice him once or twice in the village, often doing the shopping. On those occasions, I had no cause to worry about him. Jenny, his daughter-in-law, had obviously decided that he liked something to do and knowing that he did love Aidensfield, she'd realized that a long walk to fill a shopping bag with essentials from the village shop was an excellent way of keeping the old man occupied, both mentally and physically. He could even visit the pub for a chat with some of his old pals and Margot did say they had been asked to keep an eye on him too. Having spotted him in the village with the shopping bag, I did not interfere, knowing that if he did not return to the farm within a certain time, I'd receive a telephone call. But I didn't receive any such calls because old Mr Chesterfield always returned to the farm with his load intact.

As time passed, it seemed he was settling happily into his former home at High Newbiggin Farm and everyone—family, Margot and myself—began to feel that his aimless wanderings had ceased. But they hadn't. After a few months, he started to wander away from the premises. For some reason, old Mr Chesterfield's mind would suddenly develop a fault and off he would go, wandering away from home at all hours of the day and night without knowing where he was heading or why he was leaving.

There were times he'd left in the early hours of the morning dressed only in his pyjamas, times when he'd dressed in his Sunday best but instead of going to church he'd gone into the woods to pick mushrooms, times when he'd told the family he was going to meet a friend in the pub when in fact he'd wandered across the open moors with a vague expression on his face. Once he'd got out of bed at midnight to muck out the cow house and feed the hens. In most of the cases, the family very quickly became aware of his absence and were able to trace him and return him to the fold without too much trouble. But even during those excursions, his appearance was one of a perfectly normal old gentleman. A casual observer would never realize the fellow had a mental problem.

Once or twice, however, when his family were unable to trace him, I did get a worried phone call as a result of which I had to mount a low-key search of the district. And on every occasion, I, or someone who knew him well, managed to locate the lonely wanderer and take him home. He never went very far away. To give him due praise, he never tried to avoid being returned to the farm and, to be honest, he seemed to have no idea of his whereabouts or even his identity until he walked through the door, when his memory seemed to click back into working order. And then he was perfectly normal again. Familiar surroundings did appear to settle his mind and give him comfort.

It was all very sad and potentially dangerous for old Mr Chesterfield, but Margot said this kind of thing could happen to elderly folks. In most cases, the entire population of the village took it upon themselves to look out for any aged wanderers who happened to live among them and to inform their relatives or help in other ways. Mr Chesterfield was no exception but one pleasing factor was that the people of Aidensfield would care for him as well as his family and the professionals—even if he wandered along the road to Ashfordly, someone would notice him and return him home. That kind of local support was reassuring to all. It did seem, however, that one remedy was to keep old Mr Chesterfield in the vicinity of the farm and to ensure he was fully occupied—that combination of factors also meant he could be supervised. With the experience of a few months at the farm, it became evident that while he was gainfully occupied, he would never stray from his home pastures. He wandered when he was bored.

Alan and Jenny were determined to ensure that he had something to occupy him every hour of the day and it was fortunate that the one thing of which he never tired, was the sight and sounds of the routine of the farm. He was quite content to sit and watch the cows being milked or the sheep being clipped. He liked to help feed the calves or gather in the eggs and would even give a hand with the mucking out in either the pig sties or the cow sheds.

In short, his return to the farm had appeared to improve his mental state and at the same time had given him some happiness in his declining years. Alan and Jenny's response had been successful because there is no doubt that as time went by, the frequency of his wandering began to decrease. The time had almost arrived when he could be trusted to stay alone on the farm, if only for a short time.

Then one autumn day, Jenny had to represent Aidensfield Women's Institute at an event in York. It was an annual meeting of representatives from all the Women's Institutes in Yorkshire. It was an important occasion and one at which Aidensfield should be represented. Jenny had been chosen for the task which meant joining the bus which collected other delegates from nearby communities; it would collect her outside the post office at 9.45 a.m. and she expected to return at 6 p.m. or thereabouts. It so happened that Alan's only workman, a general labourer called Ike Wilson, was ill with flu that day which meant that Alan would be alone on the farm. Under normal circumstances, that would not create a major problem, but the question of keeping an eye on old Mr Chesterfield arose. Although the need had considerably reduced, Alan continued to be concerned about his father and wondered if he could cope with the old man for the whole of that Wednesday while completing his own tasks.

One of the fields had to be ploughed, the soil needed to be turned so that the frosts of autumn would work the earth and reduce it to a rich loam; the field in question, a massive hillside patch on the edge of the moor, would take all day and possibly more to plough, even using a tractor instead of horses.

Alan, knowing of his father's delight at seeing newly ploughed land with long, shining furrows and symmetrical patterns on the landscape, decided he would invite his father to watch him turn the earth. That way, he could keep the old fellow under modest if rather distant supervision. Alan would take a packed lunch and flasks of coffee for their 'lowance times and, in some ways, it would remind Mr Chesterfield of his own days at the farm.

When Alan mentioned it to his father, Mr Chesterfield thought it was a wonderful idea. He said he would really enjoy watching the seasonal ploughing, to say nothing of the wildlife he would observe at the same time.

'It's a nice idea, but where will you put him so he can watch what's going on, Alan?' Jenny had asked. 'You'll have to keep him interested all day.'

'I'll put him in my car,' Alan had told her. 'I'll park it in that top pasture; it overlooks the field I'll be ploughing and if he sits in the front passenger seat, he'll get a really good view. There's a radio in the car too; it'll be comfy and warm, and he can put the heater on if he gets cold. I'll join him for my breaks, so he'll have company for part of the day and it won't seem as if I am keeping him under close scrutiny. That should please him!'

And so the plan was put into operation. Old Mr Chesterfield warmed to his part in the day's ploughing. He could take the newspapers too, or a book, and his packed lunch, and something for ten o'clocks and three o'clocks, a flask or two of coffee, and even a bottle of whisky ... 'I'll be fine, Alan,' he had smiled. 'Let Jenny go to her WI, we'll be grand you and me, just the pair of us up there.'

That Wednesday in October, Jenny put on her best clothes and Alan drove her down to the village to catch the bus, then returned to put his own plans into action. When he got back, his dad was waiting with enough luggage to supply a holidaymaker for a fortnight, but Alan allowed the old man to pack it all into the car. He'd even brought a pack of cards in case he wanted to play patience, and a holdall containing a change of clothing in case he got soaked while taking a stroll in the field. Clearly, Mr Chesterfield was taking this outing very seriously.

The previous evening, as part of his preparations, Alan had parked the tractor and plough in a barn in a corner of the field so it was in position for the day's work; all he had to do was drive his car along the grassy lane and park it in the prearranged place with his father on board. This he did. Leaving his dad in the passenger seat, he parked it facing south-east where it had extensive views across the field in which he would be working.

'There you are, dad,' he said. 'You can have a grand time here. I'll leave the keys in the ignition—if you want me for anything, switch it on and pip the horn. And if you want the heater to work, you'll have to switch it on and run the engine for a few minutes to warm it up. Now this is the radio ...'

'I can work the controls of a car, Alan, I used to have one. I taught you to drive, remember! I'm not senile, you know!' Vincent had snapped. 'Now off you go and get started, otherwise you'll not get finished before dark. I'll be fine ... I've brought enough to keep me occupied for months! I can even camp out a couple of nights if I have to. So forget me and get on with what you're supposed to be doing.'

And so Alan left his father sitting in the car as he went to start the tractor and commence his own work. From time to time while ploughing, Alan looked across to the hillock upon which the car was parked, and saw his father's figure inside. He was sitting quite still, reading, listening to the radio or simply watching the progress of the work in the fields. On one occasion, he went for a short walk but returned to the car within five minutes. His return pleased Alan—Dad seemed to be acting sensibly. Then Alan halted his labours about half past ten and joined his dad in the car for coffee break. They'd have drinks and a scone—'lowance as it was known locally.

For a few minutes, the two men chatted about farm work and Alan found himself enjoying his dad's companionship. All too soon it was time to resume. Alan returned to his tractor with a promise that he would knock off for lunch about 12.30 and rejoin Dad in the car. Mr Chesterfield said he was fine, he'd tackle the *Yorkshire Post* crossword, find something on the radio to listen to and maybe stretch his legs with a longer walk down to the stream. Alan signified his agreement. It seemed that Dad was not going to be a problem today.

About three-quarters of an hour later, when Alan was completing a somewhat complicated turn at the far end of the field, he glanced towards the place he'd left his car—but it had gone! At first, he couldn't believe his eyes. He thought his position at the distant end of the field had obliterated his view so he halted the tractor and leapt from it to run to a higher position. But the car was not there. And neither was Dad.

He recalled his father saying something about going for a walk beside the stream, but he wouldn't have taken the car down there—access was via a narrow footpath. With the tractor engine still running, Alan wondered whether it would be quicker to unhitch the plough and take the tractor in pursuit of the car, or simply run to the farmhouse to see if Dad was there. After all, he might have gone to the toilet.

The wisdom or otherwise of letting the old man sit in a car with the keys in the ignition now came into question but Alan found himself running almost a mile to the house to see if his father was there. Panting heavily, he arrived but saw the car wasn't parked near the house or in the outbuildings. Alan ran into the house, shouting 'Dad, are you there?' but there was no response. He checked the bathroom, the downstairs toilet, the kitchen, his father's own end of the house, then all the bedrooms and lounge. Finally, he rushed around the outbuildings calling his father's name, but there was no sign of him. With a feeling of absolute dread, he had to accept that both car and old man had vanished.

That's when he rang my police house. I was out on patrol but Mary managed to get a message to me via the police radio, and

I went straight to High Newbiggin Farm. It was around noon when I arrived having first done a swift but unsuccessful search of the village for the old man and Alan's car which I knew by sight even if I did not remember its registration number. By the time I arrived at the farm, Alan was pacing up and down the yard, the anxiety now clear on his face.

'I just don't know where he could have gone, Nick.' He swept his hand through his thick hair. 'I've looked everywhere, inside and out, and he's not here. He's got the car, though, that's the problem, and it's packed with enough stuff to see him through a holiday! Spare clothes, the lot! In a holdall. I should have realized he was plotting something, the cunning old devil!'

'Have you any idea where he might have gone?' I asked.

'If he's not in the village, no. I've no idea,' Alan admitted.

At this point, he told me the complete story behind this escapade along with his father's background, and I sympathized with him, expressing hope that old Mr Chesterfield would not come to any harm. He might voluntarily return to the farm but nonetheless, I said I would initiate a formal search. I made a note of Mr Chesterfield's description and the clothes presently being worn by him, along with a more detailed description of the car and its registration number. Armed with this information, I radioed force control room to ask that observations be maintained for the car and its driver.

'Is there a particular area of search?' asked the operator from control.

I looked at Alan who was with me as I made this appeal and he said, 'He used to take my mum to Scarborough for the day, and he did live there for a time in retirement. He does love Scarborough, it's the only place I can suggest.'

I relayed this to control who said they would make an especial request to all mobiles patrolling the coastal areas, and details would be passed to the town police of Scarborough.

Several of the Scarborough officers knew Mr Chesterfield by sight, having located him on previous occasions, but the fact he was in a car would make the search slightly more difficult in a busy seaside town. There'd be thousands of cars in the town at this time of year—once the school holidays were over, the older folks descended upon the resort for a long, quiet holiday. But everything that could be done would be done and I did make the point that Mr Chesterfield had left Aidensfield less than an hour ago, consequently he could still be *en route* to the coast.

Control said that two patrol cars were currently on the main road between Ashfordly and Scarborough; they would be asked to monitor all motor vehicles travelling towards the coast. If Mr Chesterfield had chosen that route, which was the most direct from Aidensfield, he would surely have to pass one or other of the police vehicles. They would stop and quiz him if he was found, and he'd be asked to remain until collected by a member of his family. I agreed with that logic, and added a further point by saying that Vincent Chesterfield had loaded the vehicle with luggage this morning.

It was quite feasible he might decide to spend the night in the car or head off for bed-and-breakfast accommodation somewhere, possibly at Scarborough. Having set in motion a search by all patrolling officers, I promised Alan I would make a further, more diligent search of Aidensfield

126

and the nearby villages. Alan wanted to help me in my search but I suggested he remain at the farm, close to the telephone in case he was required by us, or of course, by his escaped father. He said he would do that—ploughing would have to be abandoned for today.

He did add, though, that he was unsure how much petrol the car contained. He had not filled the tank for several days, and had not checked the gauge this morning. If it was nearly empty, the old man might run out of fuel somewhere and be stranded. I said I would bear that in mind—if he was not located by teatime, I could revive interest by suggesting the car had been abandoned somewhere, having run out of fuel.

Having done what I could at the farm, including my own careful search of the house, outbuildings and nearby lanes or fields, I left the premises and first checked all his usual haunts in Aidensfield—the shop, post office, pub, churchyard where his wife was buried, friends' homes, but old Mr Chesterfield had not been seen this morning. Then I called at the garage and learned he had filled up the car—and he'd put the cost on his son's account. So he had a car *and* a full tank of petrol!

'Did he say where he was going?' I asked Edwin, the Aidensfield garage owner.

'He said he was having a day out,' responded Edwin. 'He didn't say where.'

'And did he look all right? Not ill? No glazed look about him?'

'No, he looked perfectly all right to me,' he assured me. 'He had some luggage in the car and the radio was going full blast. He looked very happy, Nick, I'd say. And he seemed really pleased he was having a day out.'

'He did say a *day* out? Not a holiday or a weekend away?'

'No, day out. That's what he said when he signed the chit. He was having a day out, those were his exact words.'

'What time did he call in?' I asked.

'Can't say for sure, Nick, but not long ago. Less than an hour, I'd say.'

'Thanks, Edwin,' I said.

I was now convinced that old Mr Chesterfield was on his way to Scarborough, just like he had done in the past. I could imagine he was re-enacting one of his happy outings when he had taken time off from his busy farming schedule to spend a day at Scarborough with his wife. I went to my house and rang Alan at the farm to update him and then rang Ashfordly police to ask for a close search of other villages in the Ashfordly area. If Mr Chesterfield was anywhere in the countryside which was policed by Ashfordly Section, we would trace him.

But we didn't.

The only consolation so far as Alan was concerned, was that no traffic accidents had been reported, no old men had been admitted to local hospitals suffering from loss of memory or other ailments and injuries, and his own car had not been found empty and abandoned anywhere. This suggested that old Mr Chesterfield was still aboard and driving it.

After my own search produced nothing I could sense the anguish being suffered by Alan Chesterfield. I knew he would be frustrated at not being able to involve himself actively in the hunt for his missing father, and yet, from past experience, I knew that the only hope lay in some police officer coming across the old character and his car. In that sense, a lot of luck was involved—missing car and searching police officer had to be in the right place at the right time, otherwise they would miss one another.

I did know that, where old folks are concerned, the police do make a special effort to ensure their safety. I had every faith in my colleagues. But by teatime, there was still no sign of old Mr Chesterfield or the car. Both Ashfordly police and the force control room maintained contact with me, providing regular updates on their activities which I relayed to Alan by telephone. Sadly, they were all negative. I continued to patrol the Aidensfield area, extending my search to out-of-the-way places and old haunts of Vincent, even dating back to his courting days thanks to information from his son, but he was not at any of those locations. He seemed to have disappeared from the face of the earth.

The next problem was the onset of darkness and with it, a chilling of the atmosphere as night set in. If the old man had got lost or if his car had broken down in some remote place, he'd have to spend the night in the cold and although a car does offer some protection against the weather, it is not a very satisfactory place in which to spend a chilly night.

I went up to the farm to see Alan, chiefly to reassure him that the police were doing everything possible—they'd arranged several special visits to the seafront at Scarborough, checking the car-parks and streets for the car. They even sent an officer around the hotels and some of the more popular boarding-houses but Vincent Chesterfield was not among their guests and his car was not in their car-parks. I did my best to reassure Alan that his father was safe—we'd have known if he'd been involved in an accident or had collapsed or had entered hospital, but by this time Alan was almost distraught. As I sat with him in his farmhouse kitchen, a car pulled up outside.

'That'll be Jenny back,' he said upon hearing the engine. 'She's about due. She said she'd get a lift from the village when she got back. God knows what I'll tell her—she told me to keep an eye on Dad, and look what's happened ... a lost dad and a lost day's work ...'

The kitchen door opened to admit someone, but it wasn't Jenny. It was old Mr Chesterfield and he was clutching an armful of items he'd brought in from the car.

'Dad!' there was a mixture of relief and anger in Alan's voice as he rose to his feet. 'Where the hell have you been? We've been worried sick ... there's been a search, the police, the villagers, Mr Rhea ... everybody.'

'I had a day out,' he said quite calmly. 'A lovely day out just like I used to do. I don't have to get your permission to have a day out, do I, Alan? I am a grown man, you know, and I'm not senile.'

'Have you any idea of the alarm you've caused?'

'Can you help me unload the car?' smiled Mr Chesterfield, totally ignoring his son's protests. 'I did have a nice picnic lunch.'

'What can I do?' Alan looked at me with exasperation all over his face. 'What can I do with the silly old buffer?'

'Where did you go?' I asked Mr Chesterfield.

'It was just like the old days,' he said. 'I went through all the lanes, all the byways and little villages, looking at fields and farms and cows and sheep, making notes, comparing them with my own farm, you know, like I used to do. Farmers do like to see how other farmers arc going about things. You learn from them that's better than you. And there's some fine buildings out there, Alan, big modern barns and some nice dry stone walling but there's a chap over by Eltering has no idea about harvesting and another chap has let his field get full of poppies; they're a bit late, I reckon, getting harvested. There's some ploughing now and I saw a fox over by Brantsford, near that watersplash ...'

'So you didn't go to Scarborough?' interrupted Alan.

'Well, I intended going, but there was so much to see on the way, and I had a cup of tea with such a nice lady at a farm over by Slemmington who keeps some Highland cattle I was looking at, and when I popped into Eltering Mart I thought the sheep weren't up to scratch.'

'Mr Chesterfield,' I said, 'if you want to have a day out, I'm sure Alan would never object, but you must tell him where you are going and what time you'll come back. That's only fair to him and Jenny—and to me and my colleagues. We've spent a lot of time and money looking for you today.'

'If I'd asked him if I could go by myself, he'd have said "no",' retorted the old man. 'So I decided, on the spur of the moment, to have a day out. I can do that without asking anyone, can't I? I am not a child, Mr Rhea. I am not senile. So if I want to go out, I shall go, without asking permission of anybody. And I'll come back, like I have today.'

'All right, but can I ask you to let Alan know when you decide to go?' I put to him. 'That isn't asking permission to go, it's saying you are going, so we're not looking all over Yorkshire for you.'

He looked at me steadily and then at Alan, and said, 'Sorry, Alan. I'm not used to asking permission to do things ... but I will tell you in the future, if I decide to have a day out. I promise.'

'Thanks Dad,' and Alan stepped forward to put an arm around his father, the first show of emotion I had ever witnessed in him. 'Come on, let's get that car unpacked before Jenny gets home, otherwise we'll both be in bother!'

As the old man pottered upstairs with some of the things he had already brought in, Alan said to me, 'Sorry about all this, Nick, but I was worried about him.'

'Don't worry,' I said. 'You did the right thing. I'll tell our people that he has returned safe and sound but I think we've all learned something from this.'

'Have we?'

'Well, I wonder if your dad has ever been allowed out on his own in recent times? Maybe he should be given more freedom ... not less. And he has shown two things to us today.'

'What are they?' Alan asked.

'That he knows his way home, and that he regards this place as his home. I think both are very important.'

'Yes, they are. You're right. Thanks Nick.'

'I'll go and leave you two to work something out,' I said, and as I left, I heard a car coming along the track towards the farm. Jenny was being brought home, and I wondered what they would tell her. But it was nothing to do with me, not any more.

The other old gentleman to whom I referred at the beginning of this chapter adopted an equally dramatic way of drawing attention to his plight and, like old Mr Chesterfield, he kept disappearing from home. But in addition to his disappearing act, he had another trick in his repertoire, a very expensive one.

He was called Jacob Bolton and in his younger days, he had owned a highly successful transport business, specializing in furniture removal but undertaking the long-distance carriage of other heavy goods. Jacob, a very shrewd businessman, had built his business from scratch, starting with an old second-hand lorry. He had bought others as his business improved, quickly moving to new vehicles when he could afford it and eventually, he had a huge fleet of the most modern of heavy goods vehicles. There is no doubt he had made a lot of money but he had earned it. Before retiring, he had handed the running of the business to his two sons and only daughter, then after a period as chairman of the company, he had retired to leave them with that responsibility. The business, and the worries of running it, were now theirs. That had been his ambition as a young, hard-working entrepreneur—to establish his business so soundly and with such efficiency that it would support all his family when he decided to retire. And so it did.

His children were equally as efficient and hard-working as their father had been, with the Harrowby-based Bolton Transport being the recognized leader in its field. In his retirement, Jacob and his wife, Betty, had sold their home at Harrowby and had come to live at Aidensfield. They bought a large stone-built detached house on the outskirts of the village.

It overlooked the dale and boasted a large garden which he and his wife tended; there were two greenhouses and a conservatory, with privet hedges, a goldfish pond and extensive lawns. The fine and spacious interior with some oak-panelled rooms was furnished with antiques and oil paintings and he had two cars in the garage, a beautiful Jaguar and a solid Rover. In many ways, the life of Mr and Mrs Bolton seemed to be perfect—after a hard and successful business career, they were enjoying retirement to the full. Then Betty Bolton died. Quite unexpectedly she suffered a massive heart attack and was dead before she reached hospital. Jacob was devastated and for a few months afterwards, seemed to live the life of a recluse, but in time the wounds healed and he reappeared, sometimes popping into the pub for a few whiskies which he enjoyed with his cigars, or else going off to one or other of the racecourses which graced the North Riding of Yorkshire. For a man in his early eighties, he led an active and busy social life, even if he was alone.

But, I was to learn, his private life was one of utter solitude and loneliness. When he went into his fine house, he had no one to visit him. No one called on him. Following Betty's death, his interest in the house began to wane and soon the garden was overgrown. The house began to appear neglected. It needed a coat or two of paint and although Jacob was unable to perform those chores in person, he did have the money to pay others. But he did not do that. He let himself go, as the locals put it. Whenever he appeared in public, his clothing looked unkempt, his hair was untidy and his fine cars were always dirty. Money was not a problem, however.

He always had a pocket full of £1 and £5 notes and he paid cash for most of his purchases in the shop, garage or pub. He never ran up debts and was regarded as an ideal customer by all the Aidensfield businesses.

And then he disappeared. It was Gilbert Kingston, the postman from Elsinby, who raised the alarm. Due to changes in the postal delivery service, Gilbert now delivered mail in both Elsinby and Aidensfield and at half-past eight one morning, he hurried to my door.

'Nick,' he said, 'I'm worried about old Jacob. All his doors and windows are standing open, his Jag's gone from the garage, and he's nowhere in the place. I shouted and had a look around, but he's gone. It's deserted.'

'I'll come and have a look,' I assured him.

Jacob's home was only a five-minute walk from the police house and, with Gilbert accompanying me, I soon arrived. I found the front door standing wide open with the ground-floor windows of the lounge and dining-room also open. The garage doors were also standing wide with an empty space where his sky-blue Jaguar was normally parked. The immediate impression was that Jacob had left with tremendous haste, but policemen tend to be very cautious about superficial appearances.

'I'll need to look around the house and outbuildings,' I said to Gilbert. 'Garden too, anywhere he might be. He could have been attacked and had his car stolen, or he might have had a brainstorm of some kind. I'd like you to accompany me.'

Together, we searched the entire house and grounds but there was no sign of Jacob. On the kitchen table, there was a plate bearing some crumbs of toast and a mug containing the remnants of coffee; when I felt the electric kettle, it was still warm.

'He hasn't been gone very long,' I told Gilbert.

'He's never left the house open like this before,' the postman told me. 'He often used to tell me if he was going off for the day, and when he did go away, he always locked up.'

'I'll call his sons,' I said. 'They might know where he's gone.'

To save time, I used Jacob's own telephone and rang Bolton Transport at Harrowby. After identifying myself, I asked for either of the sons or Jacob's daughter. My call was put through to Kenneth Bolton who was already in his office. I explained what had happened and asked if he had any idea where his father might have gone, or why he would rush out of the house and leave the doors and windows standing open.

Kenneth responded but there seemed

little concern in his voice, 'Sorry, no, Mr Rhea. It's most uncharacteristic of him to do that. He did ring yesterday and gave no hint of any problems; he sounded his usual self, a bit grumpy but quite sensible. He'll have run out of tea or coffee or something. Have you tried the shops?'

'Not yet, I'm speaking from his house; we've just discovered his absence. If he has gone out and if he isn't at the shops or in the village, where might he be? Any ideas?' I asked him.

'I haven't a clue,' he responded.

I tried again. 'What I mean is—if he's got a problem of some kind and has gone to think it over, where would he go?'

'The only problem he's had in recent years is the death of my mother,' Kenneth explained. 'He was devastated by that. I don't think he's fully recovered in spite of the good show he puts on for us all. So if he has gone anywhere to cry or be miserable, then it would be somewhere that meant a lot to both of them.'

'Any suggestions?' I got the impression I was having to drag this information out of Kenneth Bolton.

'It's difficult to say,' he sighed. 'They did their courting on the moors; he had a bike then. He and mum would cycle from here up Sutton Bank and look at the view from the top, he often talked about that. She did, too. They'd sit and look down on Lake Gormire. And Byland Abbey ... Rievaulx Abbey, they'd cycle there. They were their favourite places ... Look, Mr Rhea, what happens next? Will there be publicity?'

'Well, first, I shall search Aidensfield and the locality. I'll check at the shops and garage, and all the usual places, including the doctor and nurse. But if no one knows where he is, I'll have to consider a full-scale search with calls to the local hospitals. That might attract publicity. In fact, publicity could help to trace him if he's wandered off.'

'Shall I come over to Aidensfield?' he suggested. 'I could be there in, say, forty minutes.'

'Give me time to check around the village first,' I advised him. 'That'll take me an hour or so. I'll ring you back with the outcome of that, and we'll take it from there.'

'You don't think he's had burglars or been kidnapped, do you?' Kenneth was clearly starting to think the worst. 'He

142

does keep a lot of cash on him and in the house.'

'It doesn't look as though the house has been searched by villains,' I assured him. 'It has all the hallmarks of a hurried departure.'

'He'll have run out of cigars or something!' said Kenneth.

'Let's hope that's all it is,' I responded. 'But I'll ring in about an hour.'

Gilbert and I left the house, closing the doors and windows without locking them. Gilbert said he would continue his rounds but at the same time ask if anyone had seen Jacob this morning, and I said I would begin my enquiries in Aidensfield. I did have a little success—Jacob Bolton had gone into the shop shortly after eight this morning to buy a box of cigars and some matches. The shopkeeper, Joe Steel, had noticed the Jaguar parked outside with the engine running, and had assumed Jacob was hurrying off to a meeting of some kind. But Jacob had not commented upon his intended destination; carrying his newly purchased cigars and matches, he'd returned to his car and driven off with a roar of its distinctive sounding exhaust. Joe said that, in his opinion, Jacob was in good health and fine spirits. Certainly, he was not depressed or showing signs of worry or illness. Although I continued my questions within the village, no one else had noticed Jacob's departure.

I encountered Gilbert Kingston during my enquiries and told him what had transpired; he, on the other hand, had not gleaned any useful information from his customers and so I returned to my house to inform Sergeant Blaketon of my endeavours and to ring Kenneth Bolton with an update.

When I spoke to Blaketon, he asked, 'So what are your proposals, Rhea? A big search, a local search or no search at all?'

'I think a local search is called for, Sergeant,' I suggested. 'I have to ring his son now, at Harrowby, and I was going to suggest that he and I meet, and that he takes me to the places his father is likely to visit. If he's not there, and if he hasn't turned up by lunchtime, we could launch a wider hunt.'

'There is no reason to believe he is in danger, is there?' he asked.

'Not in my opinion, Sergeant,' I said, hoping the old man had not committed suicide.

'Right, do that. And let me know how things progress.'

When I rang Kenneth with my news, he readily agreed to meet me. Any further calls for the family could be relayed through the staff at the depot. I suggested the car-park at Sutton Bank Top as a rendezvous point. We could then both explore the area and deal with whatever we discovered. I said I would be at Sutton Bank Top at 10.15 a.m. and he promised he would be there. I was first to arrive and the first thing I found on the car-park was Jacob's distinctive blue Jaguar. It was parked neatly and locked.

I looked around but there was no sign of its owner, so I decided to await Kenneth's arrival. He came in a large Volvo estate car and crossed immediately to me, introducing himself with a strong handshake. He was about a good six feet tall, fifty years of age I estimated, with grey hair, smartly dressed in a dark business suit. He was a younger version of his father.

'That's Dad's car,' he said slowly, walking around it, trying the doors and looking inside. 'He can't be far away.'

'So where do you think he's gone?' I asked.

'Once, he would have climbed down to

145

Lake Gormire,' he smiled. 'But he's a bit old for that now, the climb through those trees is a bit steep for old folks. I reckon he'll have gone the other way, towards the gliding club airfield and the Kilburn white horse. There used to be a seat along there, he and Mum would sit and gaze across the Vale of York, to the Pennines and Yorkshire Dales.'

'Let's go,' I suggested.

Quarter of an hour later, we found Jacob. He was sitting on a wooden seat at the cliff top and gazing across the expansive view before him while smoking one of his huge cigars. He had no idea we were approaching from his right. I saw him take a long drag on the cigar, savour the scent and the smoke, then raise his head slightly to blow the smoke into the sky. It rose in a tiny cloud to be dissipated by the prevailing winds on that hill top. We walked towards him on the grassy track. There was no one else on this path at that time of the morning, and then he became aware of our approach.

'Hello, Dad,' said Kenneth.

'Oh, you've come to see me, have you?' was the slightly sarcastic reply. It was then that I noticed the bits of charred paper

146

lying on the ground around the seat. He'd been lighting his cigars with the papers instead of matches and his box of cigars lay open on the seat at his side.

'Hello, Mr Bolton.' I felt I had to say something.

'Been looking for me, have you?' He grinned wickedly at me.

'Yes, your house was found with all the doors open and we were worried.'

'There's no need to worry on my account, Constable. I'll not jump off this cliff or do anything daft—except light my cigars with five-pound notes.'

And then I realized what the pieces of burnt paper were. They were the charred remains of £5 notes.

'Dad, you bloody fool!' snapped Kenneth. 'What's all this about?' He rushed forward to pick up some of the pieces.

'I'm going to burn all my money.' He grinned even more wickedly at Kenneth. 'I slaved for you and the others,' he said. 'You got my business and when I die, you'll expect to get my money. But you never come to see me, any of you. Neither you nor William nor Ruth have been to see me in the last three months, not one of you. Now you know I like a cigar, and

I like a glass of whisky, so I'm going to buy myself the very best whiskies and the very best cigars. I shall drink the whisky and use my money to light my cigars, here on this seat, or somewhere else. What else is there for me?'

'Dad!' Kenneth's voice softened. 'Dad, we do come to see you, we love you but we're very busy ... you know how hectic it is, running a business like ours, weekends and weekdays alike. You did it ...'

'But I always went to see my mum and dad,' he said. 'And I made time for you as kids, and I made time for them when they were old.' And as if to emphasize his point, he pulled a £5 note out of his pocket, lit it with a match and applied it to the end of his cigar which had gone out while he was talking. He drew on the cigar until it was glowing again, threw the remains of the fiver to the ground and stamped on it to put out the flames.

'Another one gone,' he grinned, puffing a cloud of smoke into the cool air.

'Look, Dad, let's go home and talk about this.'

'There's nothing to talk about,' he said. 'So long as I am left alone at weekends, I

148

shall light my cigars with £5 notes. I don't need that amount of money any more. And I do enjoy a good cigar with a Yorkshire view spread before me.'

I decided this was no longer anything to do with me and said, 'Look, Kenneth, I'm leaving. Your father is safe and this is a family matter. I am not involved any more.'

'There will be no publicity about this, will there?' Kenneth looked worried. 'I mean about dad lighting his cigars with fivers.'

'No,' I said. 'It's between you and your father now.'

'I might decide to light my next lot of cigars on top of York Minster,' chuckled Jacob.

'You wouldn't dare!' snapped Kenneth.

'Try me,' grinned his father. 'And if I do, I might just ring the papers. They'd like that, wouldn't they? An eccentric old man in York Minster lighting his cigars with fivers ...'

And I left them, radioing to Sergeant Blaketon to say that Jacob had been found safe and well. I told him the story and he chuckled.

'Let's hope they decide to visit him more

often,' he said. 'It'll cost them a lot if they don't!'

But Jacob did resort to his cigar lighting ruse on more than one future occasion, each time vanishing from home after a lonely weekend, and each time he was found on that seat near Sutton Bank Top, the place he had courted his wife.

But someone always collected the remains of the burnt fivers. It helped to keep that beauty spot free from rubbish, but I have no idea who it was.

4 The Best Laid Plans

So many schemes thou breedest.
Matthew Arnold (1822–1888)

When I arrived at Aidensfield as the village constable, I was fortunate to inherit a wealth of material left by my efficient predecessor. There were the expected notes which related to my duties, such as lists of farms and farmers, public houses and landlords, garages, shops, post offices and other business premises in the villages on my patch but in addition, he left me notes about some of the personalities on the beat. This rather comprehensive file included a list of convicted offenders and those who were known to commit crime, even if they had never been caught. There was a section on poachers too, in which the names of Claude Jeremiah Greengrass and his dog Alfred featured with some prominence. My predecessor's work and his foresight in leaving me so well equipped for my duties has long been appreciated.

But among the papers was a sketch plan of some crossroads in the hills above Elsinby. I knew the place. The crossroads created a black spot, one of several places in the North Riding of Yorkshire where traffic accidents occurred with monotonous regularity. Depicted on a flat piece of paper, the location did not appear to be particularly dangerous, but in fact the layout of the roads at that point was far from perfect. A busy B-class road carrying traffic out of the hills towards York climbed from Elsinby for almost two miles. In doing so, it rose quite steeply across the moors and reached its highest point a few yards before it met the crossroads.

They were rather appropriately known as Grimdale Crossroads. As drivers approached that summit from Elsinby, the road ahead of them dipped suddenly—we call such hills 'switchbacks' and in many cases, the surface of the road beyond is invisible, - if only for a few seconds. In this case, the downward slope beyond the summit was perhaps a hundred yards long and dipping quite steeply until the road levelled out. The nature of this stretch made it very tempting to accelerate up the gentle slope from Elsinby to cross the summit at speed, and then motor swiftly down the other side and then along the level, straight and fairly wide road towards York. York lay some eighteen miles away. Certainly, the local drivers did this; they knew the road and enjoyed the exhilaration of the speed they could produce as they crossed that summit. Younger ones and some rather stupid older ones were heedless of the potential and sometimes unseen dangers ahead.

The real problem was that a country lane crossed that B-class road about seventy yards beyond the blind summit. It wasn't a right-angled crossing either; the lane met the main road at an angle. From the right as one drove from Elsinby, the lane entered the main road at an acute angle of some 30 degrees, crossed it and emerged at the far side at an obtuse angle of some 150 degrees. But because the main road at that point was still descending towards York it meant that the camber on the lane, on both sides of the highway, sloped away to a similar degree. To add to the problems, the surrounding landscape was rich with conifers, gorse bushes and other wild shrubs and trees, consequently there was restricted visibility from all the constituent roads.

From each of the four roads which met here, it was impossible to clearly see traffic approaching from one's left or right. In every case, there were problems, most of which could be overcome with a little caution and common sense. But even when one had spotted the traffic, it could disappear from sight, if only for a few seconds—dangerous seconds in fact. Quite literally, as one emerged from the lane on the left, it was impossible to see the summit of the hill to which I refer. To motorists emerging from that lane end, traffic coming from Elsinby was quite invisible for a few vital seconds. It meant that every person who came out of that minor road was risking a collision with something hurtling across the summit towards York. A vehicle which crossed the summit at speed had little or no chance to stop or to avoid a collision with something emerging from those lanes, from whichever side they came.

In short, the place was tailor-made for accidents. In Grimsdale's existing form, traffic accidents were inevitable and a fatality was a possibility. That was why my predecessor had left me the sketch plan. It depicted Grimdale Crossroads, or Grimdale as it was known locally, and was drawn to scale complete with road widths, gradients and destinations. Carriageway markings were shown, as were road signs, fences, trees, a bench and other roadside furniture. Accompanying the sketch was a brief note saying this plan could be copied for use whenever an accident occurred or if a prosecution for careless driving or something more serious was envisaged. Such a well-drawn and detailed sketch plan would save me hours of work when compiling reports of accidents at Grimdale Crossroads, or preparing a file for court.

And, knowing the reputation of Grimdale Crossroads, I knew that sooner or later, I would have to cope with an accident at that point. I hoped none would be fatal.

I did know, too, that the County Council highways department and the Force accident prevention department had examined the crossroads and had monitored its accident rate with a view to improving it, but to date nothing had been done. One problem, if that is the right word, was that only one fatality was known to have occurred at this point. A little girl pedestrian had been knocked down by a hit-and-run driver some thirty years earlier but I had none of the details in my own files. The problem was that a lack of fatal accidents could suggest to the office-bound pundits in County Hall that the road at this point was *not* dangerous! The *potential* for fatalities did not appear to be sufficient evidence of the need to improve the geography of a road. In Grimdale's case, after the little girl had died, the lay-out of the road had been changed slightly, with some widening of the main carriageway and clearing of the verges, but that had been thirty years earlier and it had served only to encourage traffic to go faster. Even by the sixties, more traffic was using the road and all vehicles were travelling at higher speeds. Grimdale was as dangerous then as it had been thirty years earlier.

Persuading motorists to drive carefully or to reduce their speed is never easy and one of the finest means is to position a uniformed police officer or even an empty police car in a position where they can be observed by passing drivers. For that reason, I paid frequent visits to Grimdale in uniform.

I would stand there for a few minutes merely to let my presence be noted, especially by those who regularly passed this way. I think it had some effect, even if temporarily, although several minor accidents and bumps did occur within my first few months on Aidensfield beat. On those occasions, the inherited sketch plan of Grimdale proved a most useful time-saving device.

One odd thing I did note during my frequent visits was a woman who often sat on the bench which was situated on a triangle of grass beside the crossroads. Whenever I saw her she appeared to be knitting. and sometimes sketching although she did watch every passing car, especially those heading towards her from Elsinby. The bench, sited at an angle from the main road, offered a view over the crossroads and up the slope leading to Elsinby via the dangerous summit I've already mentioned. From her seat, she commanded a first rate view of Grimdale and its traffic.

At first, I had no idea who she was. She did not appear at the same time every day, nor indeed did she turn up on a daily basis. Her appearances appeared to be spasmodic and without any purpose other than to observe the passing traffic. In time, I became accustomed to her presence on the seat as I passed that way.

She was in her mid- to late-thirties and rather plump in build. Only some five feet three inches or so in height, she had a round, pleasant face bordered by light-brown curly hair which was worn very long. It fell around her face and shoulders, and sometimes she would wear a bright coloured ribbon in it—red, yellow and green seemed her favourite colours.

Her clothing was colourful too, comprising a variety of pastel shades and she always seemed to be wearing multi-coloured blouses or jumpers and several long skirts, one over the other or perhaps covering an underslip or two. This made it seem she was wearing a crinoline. She was the sort of lady you'd expect to see on the dance floor of a Regency country house although it was clear she was not of the landed gentry class. She looked very much like an artist or someone accustomed to artistic surrounds. A musician even.

It was when I was called out to deal with yet another accident at Grimdale that

I made my first contact with the lady on the seat. A loaded lorry had been travelling along the side lane which led into Grimdale from the left when viewed from the Elsinby direction. A saloon car driven by a pensioner and his wife had been motoring from Elsinby—it had crossed the summit, swept down the far side and was heading for the crossroads as the lorry emerged from the left. Lorry and car had swerved to avoid each other but it was too late—there was a crash, the saloon car was written off, the elderly driver suffered a broken leg, cuts and bruises, and his wife had concussion. The lorry driver, shocked by the incident, was otherwise unhurt. And the lady on the bench had witnessed everything.

I discovered her name was Emma Philpin, she was married to Patrick who was a business executive in York, and she lived in a lovely home—Lavender Cottage—about half a mile from Grimdale Crossroads, along the lane to the left. She had two children, both teenage girls, and they were at boarding-school.

Having taken her name at the scene of that accident, I decided to interview her later and so I arranged to visit her at 11 a.m. on the Tuesday following the incident, so that I could obtain a full witness statement. She was a good witness who was able to marshal her thoughts with remarkable clarity, thus I was able to record in writing her version of the accident which would help us decide whether or not one or both the drivers should be prosecuted. When I submitted my completed accident report, Sergeant Blaketon said, 'I see Mrs Philpin's a witness again.'

'Is she?' I had no idea she had witnessed other traffic accidents.

'She sits on that seat at Grimdale Crossroads and waits for accidents to happen,' he said. 'Then she comes to court and gives her evidence; she's very experienced at that, Rhea. Your predecessor used her a lot. She's almost a professional witness.'

'It's the first time I've interviewed her,' I countered.

'It's the first prosecution we've had from a pile-up at Grimdale since you came to Aidensfield,' he reminded me. 'It's not easy prosecuting a driver without an independent witness, but if she's there when an accident happens, she'll be a witness for you. And a good one, Rhea. She has excellent powers of recall and is not easily flustered in the witness box.'

'She's not a troublemaker, is she?' I wondered.

'Not to my knowledge, she's never come to our notice in any other way,' he acknowledged.

'There are those who like telling tales about others. Like kids at school would do—tell-tale-tits, we called them. So is she doing this to court publicity?' I persisted. 'Is she the sort of person who likes to go to court and get their name in the paper? Or maybe she likes to get others into trouble?'

'I don't think so.' He shook his head. 'She's a bit on the quiet side if you ask me and a very nice woman, but mark my words, Rhea, if there's another accident at Grimdale when independent witnesses are required, I hope she'll be knitting on that seat. She's a bonus for us.'

His words soon came true. Within a couple of weeks, there was another accident at Grimdale Crossroads and Emma Philpin was on the seat at the time, knitting as usual. She saw everything. On this occasion, an empty bus was using the main road and it crossed the summit towards York just as a dustcart was slowly pulling out of the lane on the left. The bus swerved violently to miss the dustcart, crossed the road and ended its journey with its offside wheels in the ditch. There was no collision, no one was hurt and there was very little damage but the obvious questions were asked—suppose the bus had been full, suppose it had been a school bus carrying children, suppose it had contained invalids, suppose it had hit the dustcart, suppose the dustcart had been a petrol tanker or another bus full of people emerging from the side road ...

But officialdom did not think in those terms—it did not speculate but considered its actions from a basis of known facts.

The facts were the bus was empty, no one was injured and there had been no collision between the vehicles, thus on the list of accidents at Grimdale, this did not qualify as a serious. This meant it would not count if modifications to the road were to be considered. Nonetheless, when I submitted my accident report to Sergeant Blaketon he recommended the bus driver be reported for careless driving; Emma was a witness and I obtained a full statement from her.

But, as it happened, the superintendent decided not to proceed with a prosecution as there was no evidence of carelessness and no suggestion the bus driver had been speeding. The dustcart driver did not seem to have infringed any of the road traffic laws either, for he had stopped before entering the main road—Emma saw him do so.

He was not prosecuted. But it was another example of Emma's availability and willingness to be a witness. In the ensuing months, there were more accidents at Grimdale, some being witnessed by Emma while others happened during her absence. Perhaps the most spectacular was one which involved several cars being used by a wedding party—after a reception at the Hopbind Inn in Elsinby, the wedding party was invited to view the presents at the bride's home, a splendid farmhouse in the hills near Grimdale. As the bride's car, with white ribbons fluttering in the wind, sped across that infamous summit closely followed by a small procession of other cars, a little old man in a Morris Minor decided to emerge from the lane on the left. Upon approaching the main road, he had stopped, considered his actions, dithered, wondered, looked left and right umpteen times without making a decision, set off and changed his mind, dithered, looked left and right again, inched forward to get a better view, stopped again, pondered, worried and then engaged bottom gear for another time. At that stage, he pressed the accelerator and drove out—right into the path of the oncoming motorcade.

Ten cars, including that of the bride and groom, swerved one after the other like a railway engine and coaches following the same line. All were struggling to miss the old gentleman and his pottering car. And they all did miss him—but all of them finished that short trip in various positions on the verge, in the ditch or among the shrubs which lined the roadside. Happily, no one was injured although several passengers were rather shaken. Surprisingly, very little damage was caused to any of the cars—the old man, however, having finally decided to make his catastrophic move did not stop. He drove onwards, crossing the main road into the lane at the opposite side and somehow managing to avoid every one of those vehicles. And, once into the safe haven of the opposite lane, he continued his journey.

He did not stop. I doubt if he had any idea of the mayhem he had caused. Emma, on her seat, had seen it all and managed to obtain the registration number of the departing car. She gave it to me during my investigations of the road accident because the old man was culpable. Section 77 of the Road Traffic Act 1960 said, with relation to traffic accidents, that 'If, owing to the presence of a motor vehicle on a road, an accident occurs ... the driver shall stop ... and give his name and address ...' Thus, even if the old man's car was not involved in a collision, his duty on that occasion was to stop because, owing to the presence of his motor vehicle on a road, an accident had occurred.

In fact, several accidents had occurred although none was fatal. The old man should have stopped in accordance with the provision of the Road Traffic Act, but he did not. It meant he had to be reminded of his responsibilities—and perhaps be compelled to undertake a driving test and eyesight test. Thanks to Emma, we traced him and he was prosecuted for careless driving—and promptly decided to give up driving. I'm sure he made the right decision.

I had been concerned for Emma's safety throughout those accidents, but I think it was that particular and potentially serious situation—the mayhem that might have happened if the old man's car had been hit with a stream of others—that made me worry even more about her. If she persisted in sitting on that seat at a point where accidents happened with increasing regularity, I could envisage the time when she would become a casualty. Although her seat was some twenty yards away from the carriageway, it was well within the range of an uncontrolled vehicle, whether it was on its wheels or rolling about on its roof and sides. Even in the time since I had arrived at Aidensfield, traffic was moving more speedily, there was an increase in the volume of traffic on that road and there was an obvious risk of more accidents in the coming years. My own modest records showed there had been a 40% increase in the number of accidents at Grimdale within the last five years. Although the number of accidents had increased, however, there had been no fatalities and very few accidents which could be described as serious. Nonetheless, I did not want Emma to become a casualty. I was sure she had no idea of the risk she was taking while sitting on that seat. I decided to speak to her about it.

The opportunity came one late August afternoon after I had visited several farms in the vicinity of her cottage. I had an hour or so in hand before the end of my shift and, noting that Emma was not occupying her seat, I drove to Lavender Cottage. I was using my motor cycle at that time, but because it was a hot summer day, I was in shirt sleeves. I found her working in the garden, she was clearing some dead plants from the borders and realized she had heard the arrival of my motor bike. She came to her garden gate to welcome me. Dressed in eye-catching blue shorts, a light muslin top and sandals, she beckoned me to enter and I followed her to a stone seat in her garden. On a patio facing south, there was an iron table with iron chairs, all painted white and surrounded by tubs of flowers.

'Good afternoon, Mr Rhea,' she greeted me, with a pleasant smile full of humanity and warmth. I noticed her hands were covered in dirt from her work. 'After that hot work, I need a drink. Can I get you one? Iced orange? A milkshake?

Lemonade? Wine if you like?'

'I'm on duty, so iced orange would be wonderful.' I settled on one of the chairs and removed my crash helmet as she went into the house to fix the drinks.

I enjoyed the peace and quiet of her garden which was surprisingly spacious but very secluded; the house was bigger than I had anticipated too. On previous occasions, my visits had been in the kitchen or sometimes a small study which gave me no idea of the size of the place, but from this aspect, I could see it was a substantial building in local stone in a glorious setting. She came back with two glasses of orange with ice floating in the top and passed one to me.

'Is this a social call, or am I being called to be a witness again?' she asked, settling on the other chair. She had witnessed another accident a few weeks earlier and, like me, was awaiting the superintendent's decision whether or not to prosecute one of the drivers. In the past, I had called upon her many times to warn her to attend Eltering Magistrates Court at a certain time and date.

'A social call,' I smiled, sipping from the glass. 'Delicious!'

'So, what can I do for you?' She was accustomed to my presence and the uniform did not daunt her.

'Mrs Philpin ...'

'Call me Emma,' she invited.

'All right; I'm Nick. So, Emma, those accidents you've witnessed at Grimdale, I've lost count.'

'Eighteen this year,' she said. 'Twelve last year. That's only the ones I've witnessed. I'm not sure how many others there have been. Dozens, I'd say. Lots are never reported, people simply run off the road while swerving to miss others. I know lots occur without injuries or damage, so they are not reported.'

'I haven't the official figures with me,' I told her. 'But few of the accidents are classified as serious. Not yet, that is. One of these days, there will be a nasty one, a fatality ...'

'I know.' She looked into my eyes. 'That's why I keep my own records. I regard them all very seriously indeed. Even the minor ones, whether or not people are hurt.'

'I was thinking of you,' I told her seriously. 'I am here to suggest that you don't sit and watch the traffic.' I was coming to my point now.

'Oh, but you can't stop me!' she said. 'It's my right, my choice.'

'I know I cannot stop you, but I am concerned. That's why I am here. I do think you are putting yourself at risk.' I realized how carefully I would have to make my representation. 'That incident with the wedding cars—suppose one of them had hit you? That's the root of my concern—that you will be struck by a vehicle one of these days, something that's out of control through sheer speed. That seat of yours is in a very vulnerable position. In fact, I think it should be removed.'

'I put it there,' she told me quietly and with evident determination. 'I put it there so that I could sit and watch the traffic. There's no law to stop me, is there?'

I shook my head. 'No, of course not. It's just that I feel you are placing yourself in a dangerous position—it seems an odd thing to do, to sit by the side of the road and watch traffic race past, especially in such a potentially dangerous place.'

She did not reply for a few moments and sat with her eyes downcast. I began to wonder if I had done something to upset her but she looked up again and said, 'Nick, I sit there for a very good reason. I am looking for a hit-and-run driver.'

'I don't follow.' I was puzzled at this remark.

'You know there was a fatality here, a long time ago? More than thirty years ago, in fact. Before the war.'

'Yes, I had heard, but I don't know the details.'

'It was a little girl. Six years old. She was hit by a motor bike that came over the hilltop far too fast. It ran into her. She was sent flying with the impact and hit her head on the dry stone wall that was there then. She died instantly. Her name was Jessica Firth.'

'I see.' I wondered how she knew these details.

'She was my sister,' Emma continued softly. 'This was our family home, this very house. It became mine when my parents died, and when I married Patrick I stayed here, in my family home. In those days of course we walked to school; it was in Elsinby. We went along the road where the accidents happen. One day, a motor bike hurtled over the hill and ran into

171

Jessica. She died. I was there. I saw it all. She was walking in the side of the road, very close to the edge. The bike was too close to that verge, it collided with her and threw her against the wall. The bike ran over the verge and the rider fell off, but he picked himself up, got back on to his bike and rode off. The bike wasn't damaged and he wasn't hurt. I was too young to do anything like thinking to take his number, but I saw what happened ... all those years ago. I shall never forget it, Nick. That's why I got my dad to put that seat there, so I could sit and watch in case that same man came over the hill again. I was ten. I told Dad I wanted to see him again and get his number ... like I get the numbers of those who have accidents now. I saw his face too, Nick. He had no crash helmet, they didn't bother with them at that time. I will never forget his face. So I'm keeping watch for him Nick, and at the same time keeping records of the accidents which happen there.'

'You must have a very comprehensive list,' was all I could think of saying.

'I have, but I make use of the statistics. I send details to the authorities in the hope they will heed the accident rate and improve the road so that no one else will die.'

'I'm sorry,' I said. 'I had no idea.'

'If I die through being hit by a car, then it will be a mark in favour of changing the crossroads,' she said, eyeing me carefully. 'My death will save others.'

'That's a bit drastic!' I said, following with, 'You know that our accident prevention department has this crossroads under constant review? They have maps and an analysis of every accident that's happened there, over the years.'

'Yes, I know. I do write to them after every accident I witness,' she smiled. 'And they write me nice letters back. They don't say much though.'

'You ought to go and see the records at our headquarters,' I suggested. 'I think you would see that something is being done about this crossroads. It's not ignored, Emma. You really don't have to sit here and count accidents. But is that why you are such a good witness? You've developed a very clear memory of things.'

'I have trained myself to be a good witness,' she said. 'Because I let Jessica down by not being a good witness. Her killer got away because I did not take his

173

number, but I will recognize him if he comes this way again, either in a car or on a motor bike. That man's face will always live with me ... and he could still be alive.'

'It was more than thirty years ago.' I was gentle with that reminder.

'I know,' she said. 'I should think he'll be in his late forties now, or early fifties. I know I would recognize him. He won't have the bike of course, but I'm sure I would recognize him. And if I do, I shall come to tell you.'

'I'll be waiting,' I said, although I wondered whether we could prosecute someone for failing to stop after a road accident after such a long delay. 'But that seat ...'

'I shall always use it, Nick,' she said with determination. 'Until I find my man. You can't make me stop, it's my life's work. I must find him. But I do appreciate your concern. It means such a lot to me, that you have my interests at heart.'

'It would be dreadful if you became a victim,' I repeated for the final time.

She ignored my request and continued to use that seat. Over the years I was at Aidensfield, she became a witness for many more accidents, but she was always fair and always accurate in her evidence. Sadly she died of cancer some fifteen years after our earnest conversation, and, so far as I know, she never did find the man who had run down and killed her little sister. Grimdale Crossroads have survived, however, albeit with some modifications and improvements but her seat is no longer there. For a long time, I referred to it as Emma's Seat but when I pass that way now, it seems odd not seeing her there.

I'm sure she and her sister will be sitting together on a family bench in Heaven, safe from celestial traffic, I hope.

If I was wrong about the motives of Emma Philpin, the same might be said of someone who became a nuisance to Leonora Lackenby, the lady everyone called Nanny Lack.

Leonora, who had never married, was a retired nanny who occupied the tiniest of cottages at Crampton. She had served the Cramptons of Crampton Hall for many years, caring for the present owner, Lord Jeremy, when he was a child and more recently looking after Jeremy's own four children. It was Lord Jeremy who, as a child, had called her Nanny Lack because he could not pronounce her full name. In his adult life as Lord Crampton, Jeremy always promised he would care for his former nanny and so, when she retired and moved out of her self-contained flat in the Hall, she was given the tiny cottage beside the river, a place she had often admired. It was rent free and called Riverside Cottage; it had a long narrow lawn which led to the water's edge and Jeremy had built a summer house containing a seat so she could sit and watch the river and the wealth of wildlife it supported. She had moved there about six months prior to my arrival at Aidensfield.

In her retirement, Nanny Lack was a familiar figure around the village where she joined the WI, worked for the church and helped with charitable collections and other local matters. She would help those less capable than herself, doing a range of chores from baby-sitting for local mums to helping out at Crampton Hall when they were short of staff. She was a regular visitor to the Hall, being invited to lots of events such as the annual staff Christmas party, garden parties and so on. Lord and Lady

Crampton seemed to regard her almost as one of the family.

Many is the time I noticed her diminutive figure trotting through the village at night, having been baby-sitting or attending a function of some kind. She always seemed to be trotting—a tiny lady with thin legs and arms, she was in her late sixties and dressed in slightly outdated clothes. One of her regular outfits was a thick, long blue overcoat with a large fur collar and a pair of black boots—granny boots as the local children called them. There was no mistaking her when she was trotting about the village.

Then, one Monday morning, I received a call from her.

She was ringing from the public telephone in the village but did not want to state the nature of her business in case her conversation was overheard by someone passing the kiosk. She asked if I would call and see her. As I was about to begin my day's tour of duty, I said I'd be with her in half an hour, my first visit of the day. When I arrived, there was a welcoming fire in the grate and even though it was not long since breakfast-time, she had a pot of tea and some buns on the table.

After the preliminaries, she apologized for being so mysterious then said, 'I'm having money stolen from me, Mr Rhea.'

'By someone breaking in?' I asked, having not noticed any sign of an intruder.

'No, from the back door. I leave my money out for the milkman, he calls early you see. The night before it's due, I put it near the back door, under a plant pot. I put it there last night, Mr Rhea. Three shillings. A half crown and a shilling, there was. That meant I expected sixpence change. This morning, he left a note saying the milk money was due. I had a word with him, Mr Rhea, and told him I had left my money out—and I expected sixpence change which he hadn't left me. But he said it had all gone. So someone has stolen it, you see. They must have, mustn't they? If it's not there.'

When dealing with some people, a police officer must bear in mind their age and a possible lapse in their memory. While not wishing to disbelieve Nanny Lack, I did wonder if she had simply forgotten to put out her milk money but I had to try and establish whether or not she had really done what she claimed.

'Show me,' I invited.

Outside the back door there was a small clay plant pot standing upside down and she lifted it to show me her hiding place—and there was a half-crown and a shilling. It was her milk money, all safe and sound.

'But it's there ...' She looked at me, disbelief on her tired face. 'It wasn't there this morning, Mr Rhea. I know it wasn't.'

I was tempted to say that we all make mistakes, but instead, I said, 'Show me the note the milkman left.'

It was tucked behind the clock on her mantelpiece and she drew it out, handing it to me. In ill-formed pencil lettering on a piece of lined paper, it said, 'Milk 3/-. Stan'. In other words, three shillings was owed.

'That's how he lets me know when I forget,' she sounded apologetic. 'I don't often forget, Mr Rhea.'

'I'm sure you don't. And you didn't forget this time?' I put to her.

'No, I was most careful. I remember because I hadn't got three shillings in exactly the right money, so I put a bit extra out—three and six it was—and knew

179

he'd leave me some change. It wasn't there when he called, Mr Rhea, honestly, otherwise why did he leave the note? And I checked before I went to ring you.'

'You checked again, under the plant pot?'

She nodded. 'Yes, just in case I'd not seen it when I first checked.'

'And there was no money there?'

'That's right, Mr Rhea. There was nothing under my plant pot then. I wasn't seeing things, Mr Rhea, honestly. But it's there now ... I just don't understand ...'

In spite of her age, I was inclined to believe her. I knew that the mind can play tricks but I also knew that unpleasant people can also do despicable things to others for motives which seem inexplicable. These things happened from time to time and I hoped it wasn't happening here. It could be a solution to her problem, though.

'Has this happened before?' I asked, having returned to her table to finish my cup of tea. Sitting opposite and sipping from her cup, she hesitated for a moment and then nodded, saying, 'Yes. I must admit I wondered if I was going loopy but I'm not, Mr Rhea. I've been very careful. In this case, I am certain what I did and what happened.'

'How long has this sort of thing been going on then?'

'I moved into this cottage just over six months ago,' she said. 'I suppose the first time it happened was about three months ago. Well, what I mean to say is it was the first time I realized it wasn't me being forgetful or silly.'

'So what happened on those earlier times?'

'The insurance man comes once a month, I leave him a ten shilling note. I pay half a crown a week for some life insurance, to bury me when I go. Well, he comes every four weeks on a Friday, but I like to go to Ashfordly market on a Friday. I catch Arnold Merryweather's bus before the insurance man comes so I leave the money out for him, on the window ledge of the outside toilet. I've done it ever since I came to live here. The inside ledge, that is. I leave my book as well, he signs it when he gets the money and leaves it.'

'And what happened last time?'

'Well, I put the money out as usual, with my insurance book, on the Friday morning. The ten bob note was inside the book, tucked into the right page for him to receipt but when I got back from market, the book was still there but no money. I thought he'd been and got his money, but when I took the book back into the house and opened it, he'd put a note inside saying I'd forgotten to include the money. Then next morning when I went into the loo, the money was there, on the window ledge, all by itself.'

'The same note, do you think? Not coins?'

'It was the same note, Mr Rhea, it had an ink stain on one corner. I'd know it anywhere. It was as if someone had moved it and then replaced it.'

'Did you tell anyone about it?'

'No, what could I say? I thought it might be me going funny, getting forgetful in my old age, so I never said anything to anybody. I saw the insurance man in the street later and squared up with him and he said he was sure there was no money when he called. He said he had looked all over, including the floor in case the note had fallen off or got blown away when he moved the book. But it hadn't; it wasn't there, he was sure about that.'

She told me two more similar stories, one about money she'd left out for the Sunday newspapers and the other for a Christmas club into which she paid monthly throughout the year. In both cases, the collectors claimed she had not left out the necessary cash but then she found the money afterwards, each time in its rightful place, the very place she had left it.

'I hope you don't mind me calling you in, Mr Rhea, I'm sorry if I'm a nuisance,' she was very apologetic. 'I hope you don't think I'm going senile.'

'I'm sure you are not,' I tried to reassure her. 'The milkman's note suggests you were telling me the truth today, and the insurance man's means of receipting your book suggests the same for that occasion. So who knows where you put your money and when you leave it out?'

'Quite a lot of people, we all do it,' she said. 'We've never had bother before, Mr Rhea. Not with thieves, that is. You can trust anybody living here.'

'But your money has not been stolen, has it?' I smiled. 'What you are saying is that it's being taken away and then replaced. That's not theft—it's mischief.

183

Now why would anyone want to do something like that?'

'To make me look silly,' she said. 'To make me look daft in front of the local tradespeople.'

'So if that is the case, who would want to do it?' I pressed her.

'Are you serious?' She frowned as she looked at me over the rim of her cup. 'Do people do that sort of thing?'

'The world is full of very odd people, Leonora, and some will do some very weird things for all kinds of very strange reasons. So, is anyone jealous of you? Or have you upset anybody lately?'

She did not respond for a while and then said, 'I do know that Peggy Lapworth once had her eye on this cottage. But you mustn't even hint I said so ... she is a friend, we go to whist drives together.'

'Why did Peggy want the house?'

'She's in an estate house, Mr Rhea, in Dale Street. Number seven. Before your time, her husband worked on the estate, general maintenance side, and when he died, she wanted a smaller place. She always said she treasured this one. There was no smaller house then, and none so beautiful as this one with its riverside setting. I know she coveted the cottage, Mr Rhea, but it became vacant about the time I retired, so I got it. I didn't ask for it, by the way, I'd have been quite happy in another one, but Lord Jeremy wanted me to have it.'

'And you think Peggy was upset by that?'

'She never told me she was but I heard from other people—and she didn't speak to me for a fortnight after she knew I'd got it. I had no idea what was wrong at the time, but I found out later.'

'But she's got over it?'

'I think so—at least, I thought so until this carry-on started. I did suspect her, Mr Rhea, but didn't like to say so, with her being a friend.'

'Not a very pleasant friend, if I might say so!' I grimaced.

'She has her good points, Mr Rhea, even if she has a streak of jealousy in her. She'll always look after folks who are ill, for example, and do their shopping and washing and things. I wouldn't want to lose her friendship over this. Money's not everything and we're all a bit dishonest if we're honest with ourselves.'

I smiled at her logic and asked, 'And

185

Peggy knows where you put your money for collectors?'

'Yes, she does.' There was a look of sadness on Nanny Lack's face as she heard herself finally condemn the woman whom she had long regarded as a friend—and still wanted to keep as a friend.

'There is one snag with this tale, a legal complication,' I had to explain to her. 'If Peggy is taking the money and returning it later, she is not committing a crime. She is not stealing it because she is not permanently depriving you of your property. Legally, if she took your money and replaced it with some of her own, then technically she would have stolen your personal coins or notes even if she replaced them with the equivalent value, but I doubt if there would be a prosecution under those circumstances. But the fact that she replaces your own cash means she is not a thief, Leonora, and that means I can't prosecute her. It's a bit like borrowing, except it's done without permission.'

'I'm sure it's my own money that comes back,' she said. 'Like that ten shilling note, it was certainly mine. Does that mean you can't help me?'

'It means I can't help you officially,' I had to say. 'But I think we can give her a fright. You'd have to take the milkman and insurance man into your confidence.'

She smiled wanly and nodded her agreement.

'It would be nice to know that I'm not going daft!' she grinned. 'Honestly, there was a time I thought I was losing my marbles!'

'Right,' I said. 'I think we might prove your mind is still working properly.'

It meant I would have to obtain some crystal violet powder from our scenes of crime department and use it to coat some coins or notes which were placed deliberately so that Peggy Lapworth would remove them. I suggested that Nanny Lack should put out her money as usual in the coming weeks, say for a month, to see whether it disappeared on a regular basis. She could always pay her collectors as well and I would pop in to see if the money was disappearing as she claimed.

It was. Over the next four weeks, all her regularly placed monies were removed before being collected by those to whom they were due, and then replaced afterwards. Now, of course, Nanny Lack knew what was going on and ensured that her delivery men received their dues. When I called, I learned that Peggy Lapworth had never said anything to Nanny Lack about this and I did quiz Nanny about the likelihood of there being another suspect—but there wasn't. Indeed, Nanny had laid wait one night and had actually seen Peggy arrive under cover of darkness to remove the milkman's cash. It was time for my part in the affair.

We chose a Monday when both the milkman and the Christmas club collector were due. Nanny Lack would announce to Peggy that she was going off to Brantsford on the morning bus and would be away until teatime that day. Peggy would know that the milk money and the Christmas club money would be left in their usual hiding places by Nanny Lack. On the Sunday, therefore, having obtained the necessary crystal violet powder, I coated the milk money and the Christmas club subscription coins with a liberal coating of the powder and placed them in their hiding places. The milkman and the Christmas club collector would be paid earlier by Nanny, and would thus not have to call at Nanny's that day. There was no need to involve them in the plot.

'So what happens now?' asked Nanny, full of interest.

'If Peggy takes the money,' I said, 'her hands will become coated with the powder. She won't realize that until she puts them in water—and then they'll turn bright purple. She won't be able to wash it off—it'll last for weeks.'

'Oh, dear, poor old Peggy ...'

'It's not poor old Peggy, it's sly and scheming old Peggy,' I said. 'She's lucky she's not going to be taken to court over this! Even if it's not stealing, we might have had her bound over to be of good behaviour ... that's how we deal with nuisances.'

'Couldn't you just have a word with her?'

'I could, but she'd know you had suggested her as a likely culprit and that would cause friction between you. And I need proof of her actions before I can consider a court action—the purple hands will provide that, should I ever need it.'

'You won't interview her then?'

'For your sake, no. There is no need, not on this occasion. I might reconsider things if she does it again. But I think

189

she'll get the message this time, Nanny, I'm fairly sure of that.'

And she did.

Peggy's hands turned a bright and enduring purple colour and for a long time she refused to come out of the house. When she did emerge, a group of school children waiting for their bus noticed her and immediately called out, 'Peggy Purple Paws'. And the name stuck. But Peggy Purple Paws never misbehaved again. I avoided taking her to court and she retained Nanny Lack's somewhat cautious friendship.

5 The Grass is Always Greener

By exciting emulation and comparisons of superiority, you lay the foundations of lasting mischief.

Samuel Johnson (1709–1794)

One lunchtime, I had occasion to pop into the Hopbind Inn at Elsinby whilst I was on duty. Visiting the pub was always a pleasurable part of my routine but in this instance I wanted to combine it with a warning to George Ward, the landlord. I had news about a couple of confidence tricksters who were thought to be touring the area, fleecing the owners of boarding-houses and hotels. George was now at risk from them because he had started to use his spare rooms as bed-and-breakfast accommodation. This was an increasingly popular practice even among ordinary householders in the North York Moors now that tourism was increasing and I wished to put him on full alert.

Information received from other hotels and boarding-houses had established that their ploy was to obtain accommodation or food, or sometimes both, and then leave without paying. Sometimes they would stay for only one night although in one case they had remained a week to accumulate a substantial debt which included dinners, wine and accommodation. It was known they had run up bills in Ashfordly, Brantsford and Harrowby, invariably at the best hotels, and checks on the addresses they had logged in the hotel registers showed them to be false.

Of the couple, the man was some six feet tall and well dressed in a blazer, flannels, white shirt and striped tie; in his mid-fifties, he spoke with a cultured accent, smoked a pipe and had grey hair which was neat and well trimmed. He had a habit of opening his wallet to reveal a lot of money and speaking of his yachting holidays in the Mediterranean while mentioning famous people with whom he was acquainted. None of the swindled hotels had noticed whether or not he had a car, but his suitcase was an expensive one fashioned from the best leather. It was the showmanship of a typical confidence trickster. He was accompanied by a smart lady who was almost as tall as him; she was slim and elegant, beautifully dressed in a crisp navy-blue suit with a white blouse and black high-heeled shoes. She also spoke with a cultured accent and had beautiful blonde hair, red fingernails and wore lots of gleaming jewellery. They had all the appearances of a wealthy and trustworthy couple and had signed into the hotels as Mr and Mrs Douglas Jefferson, albeit with a variety of smart addresses, all of which were fictitious.

A couple of skilled confidence tricksters like this were very difficult to catch because they oozed charm and confidence and were quite capable of conning the most experienced of hotel or boarding-house keepers. All we could do was warn their likely victims, and so I was touring all the inns, boarding-houses and bed-and-breakfast establishments on my patch. It was during this mission, therefore, that I went into the bar of the Hopbind Inn to find a knot of countrymen enjoying a lunchtime pint. Among them was Claude Jeremiah Greengrass with his faithful companion, Alfred the lurcher.

As I entered, I could hear them

discussing horse racing but at the sight of my uniform, Greengrass shouted, 'Hey up, the law's here! Come for a pint, have you, Constable? Not that I can afford to buy you one, me being broke.'

'Not when I'm on duty Claude,' I gave the standard answer. 'Everything all right is it, George?' I turned to the landlord.

'Fine, thanks, Nick. No problems.'

'I have problems,' Claude butted in. 'Money. Or the lack of it to be truthful. I've often thought how nice it must be to get paid for coming into pubs and upsetting the drinkers ...'

'You could always get a job!' I was quite accustomed to Claude's non-stop banter. 'Getting a job is quite a good way of acquiring some money. And did you know that the harder you work, the luckier you get?'

'I reckon you can't be very lucky then!' he chuckled into his pint pot. 'So what brings you here, Constable, apart from your size twelves?'

'I'm here to warn George about people who might use his bed-and-breakfast facilities and then disappear without paying their bills.' I looked at Claude. 'Not paying for things is illegal, Claude, and I'm sure you also know that it is an offence to have alcohol on credit in a pub ... not that you would get yours on the slate, of course.'

He blinked furiously and muttered, 'Aye, well, when your income is flexible like mine is, your outgoings have to be flexible as well.'

Having completed this particular round of regular banter, I told George about the pair of confidence tricksters, provided him with the description we had been given and asked him to refuse them accommodation, and to alert me to their presence if they came to Elsinby. He promised me every co-operation, and then offered me a coffee. I accepted. It was good to talk to the local people in a pub like this and soon the locals became chatty and affable. Even Greengrass forgot his antagonism to the police and after some good natured chatter, it was he who asked George, 'This bed-and-breakfast lark, George. Is there good money to be made at it?'

'Oh aye, it's a good regular income in the holiday season,' George enthused. 'Our rooms are always full, there's always a demand. I send my overflow to farms and similar spots around here who've started doing bed and breakfast, and in return they tell the visitors to come here for snacks and evening meals. It's a popular way of touring, believe me. From my point of view, it's easier than doing full board. You've got to make sure the sheets are changed for newcomers of course, and that their room is aired and cosy, but that's it. They have breakfast and go somewhere else. The trick is to give 'em a good Yorkshire breakfast of fried eggs, bacon, black pudding, sausages, tomatoes and beans. Fills 'em up for the day. They love it, then they send their pals here.'

'And you don't have to do dinner for them? Or an evening meal? Or if it rains, they leave the place anyway? They don't hang around making it look untidy, like they do in hotels?' Claude was deliberating the merits of this scheme.

'Absolutely, Claude. No lunch, as they call it when they have summat to eat at our dinner-time, no dinner to prepare in the evening when you call it supper-time. It's a doddle, Claude.'

'And they pay cash, eh?' beamed Claude.

'Most of them, yes.'

'So what about rules and regulations?' continued Claude. 'You know, official things. Like having fire escapes and keeping hotel registers, that sort of thing.'

'Small bed-and-breakfast places, like private houses with just one or two letting bedrooms don't have to comply with all the rules which affect the larger premises, such as having fire escapes. But I think you'll need a register—all formal places, even the small ones like pubs, private hotels and boarding-houses, have some rules to comply with. You can get a copy from the council, Claude, if you're serious. And you'll have to declare the income to the Inland Revenue, for the tax man,' added George.

At the mention of the income tax man, Claude spluttered into his beer and blinked furiously at the rest of us. 'Aye, well, that's mebbe so, but I can't see somebody like me making a profit. Not summat that'll interest the tax man, I mean. Damn it, George, there's expenses to be knocked off and running costs ...'

'Fair enough, but you have to declare the income anyway, not just the profit. But why are you asking all this?' George was astounded. 'You're not thinking of going into bed and breakfast, are you?'

'Why shouldn't I?' Claude blinked

rapidly. 'I've a good-sized house with lots of space doing nowt, six bedrooms all with a rustic outlook, a farmhouse kitchen that they all yearn for these days with beams and things, and some antique furniture ...'

'And a rustic atmosphere with rusty machinery and a few very realistic farmyard aromas added for special flavour!' chuckled George.

'I can imagine a bedroom full of townies sleeping with their windows open above your midden!' chuckled one of the farmers. 'And having to use an outside nettie that hasn't got a lock on the door.'

'I don't need a lock on the door, nobody's pinched owt from my nettie. Anyroad, what I've got is just what townies like,' grinned Claude. 'They love to see us local yokels in our natural setting, a bit like a zoo. Now, if I can get 'em to stay with me, I can give 'em a true flavour of rural Elsinby, Aidensfield and hereabouts. If you send your overflow to me, George, I'll send 'em back to you for their suppers.'

'They might not want to come again!' chortled another farmer. 'You might put 'em off rural life altogether!'

'That might not be a bad thing in

198

some cases,' George responded. 'Some of them have no idea how to behave in the countryside, letting dogs out among sheep, leaving farm gates open, dropping litter, feeding the sheep with ice-creams ...'

'Aye, well, if they came to stay with me, I'd have a list of rules put up, rules of the house, about shutting gates and not giving Alfred ice-creams. They make his eyes water. I think it's the cold, getting into his teeth. He's a bit partial to fish and chips though.'

As the happy banter continued, I had to leave to keep another appointment and must admit I forgot all about this latest Greengrass enterprise. Having been to Claude's ramshackle, filthy and unkempt ranch, I could not imagine anyone wishing to spend a holiday there, however brief. One hour was more than enough; the prospect of spending a whole night or any longer period there was horrifying. Even so, he did own a very nice property which, in the right hands, would have made a delightful country house in a wonderful moorland setting. But, in the language of the estate agents of the day, it was ripe for modernization. Some might have said it was ripe—full stop!

Within a week, a notice-board appeared at Claude's gate. It was a rough wooden sign bearing in white paint the words 'Bed and Breakfast. Good rates. Vacancies. Apply Within'. It would be a few days after that, as I was standing in uniform outside the telephone kiosk in Aidensfield, that a small red and rather battered Ford Escort eased to a halt beside me. The woman passenger eased down her window. In her forties and rather plump, she hailed me with, 'Excuse me, Officer, can you tell me where Mr Greengrass lives?'

'Yes, of course,' and I gave her the necessary directions.

'I understand he does a wonderful Yorkshire breakfast,' she said.

'Does he?' Momentarily, I had forgotten all about his bed-and-breakfast enterprise and my expression of surprise alerted her.

'It is the Mr Greengrass who does bed-and-breakfast?' She examined a piece of paper in her hand and read out his address. 'Hagg Bottom?'

'There's only one Mr Greengrass in these parts, and only one Hagg Bottom,' I advised her. 'Yes, that's him, but I'd forgotten he was doing B and B.'

'He has been recommended to us by a

man we met in a pub at Ashfordly,' she smiled.

Her husband beamed up at me from his seat. 'We're from Wolverhampton, you see, we do love Yorkshire and the wide open spaces with all that fresh air. They said Mr Greengrass's house is in a very wild and romantic location.'

'Well, that's one interpretation. But I hope you find all you need at Hagg Bottom,' I smiled, reaffirming the route to the Greengrass homestead and hoping the air would be as fresh and romantic as they hoped.

I watched the car leave with a rattle of its exhaust—from the appearance of their vehicle, the couple were not very affluent and I guessed the exhaust would require renewal very soon. The tyres were fairly thin too. It was the sort of car which, if checked by an experienced traffic policeman, would probably produce a book full of faults and offences. Even though I did not check it over, I did make a mental note of its registration number, but the couple were on holiday and not harming anyone, so I never even contemplated any further action. As I watched, it chugged away with an oily smell and the woman gave me a nice smile and a wave of her hand before she closed her window. Nice, ordinary people, I decided, spending their hard-earned cash on a Yorkshire break—but at the Greengrass villa? I felt they could have received a better recommendation. There were plenty of better class bed-and-breakfast places in the nearby villages, all of a very high standard.

Any one of them would be much more pleasant than dossing down with Claude.

A couple of nights later, I was in the Hopbind Inn again, this time off duty with Mary. We were having a rare evening out together while Mrs Quarry, our regular baby-sitter, looked after the children. As we awaited our chicken-in-basket and chips, Claude Jeremiah came in and ordered a pint. This time, instead of asking for his purchases to be put on the slate, he was flourishing a pound note at George, a rare indication that he was prepared to pay on the spot. As the drink was pulled, Claude noticed Mary and I, and called, 'And one for the constable and his missus, for sending my first customers round.'

'Thanks, Claude,' I thanked him as my

pint of beer and Mary's gin and tonic arrived. 'Cheers! So how's the bed-and-breakfast business thriving?'

'Wonderful!' he enthused. 'Those folks you sent, from the smoke somewhere a way off, well, they're my sort of people. He's in second-hand metals and she's summat connected with antiques, she runs a stall on a market. Nice couple—they've ordered four brace of rabbits and two dozen fresh eggs to take home with 'em. I'll tell you what, I've told my hens to work overtime, those folks can't half knock back a good Yorkshire breakfast. Henry and Lily, they're called.'

'They like your style, then?'

'Aye, they do. So much, in fact, they decided to spend a week here. Not just one night, Constable, but six. How about that, George?' he turned and beamed at the landlord.

'Sounds like a good beginning,' returned George.

'Aye, and it's only one lot of sheets all week, no towels to need changing ... and £1 a night from each of them. Fourteen quid to come, George, more than I earn in a month ...'

'I'm pleased for you Claude,' was all I

could think of saying.

'They're not coming in here tonight, then? For their suppers?' asked George.

'No, they've gone to Eltering tonight, to the pictures, and they'll get fish and chips before they come back. They're here till the weekend. You know, Constable and George, and Missus Constable, I've right enjoyed having them, having somebody in the house to care for apart from my Alfred. I might even think of expanding—you know, building a bedroom block on the side of the house, and a special dining-room and getting a chef in, and then applying for a licence to sell booze.'

'You'll do no such thing!' snapped George. 'Bed-and-breakfast, yes: selling booze, no. That's my business, I'd object to that, I can tell you now, Claude. And you'd not be welcome in here any more, so think on that!'

'Hang on a minute!' Claude began to look flustered. 'I was just, well, talking, George, dreaming if you like, not saying what I am going to do, just what I was sort of thinking about doing ...'

'Well, so long as we know where we stand. If you apply for a liquor licence for your new establishment, Claude, I shall go to Brewster Sessions and object in the strongest possible terms. And I'd make you pay cash for all your purchases from this establishment, on the dot, on the nail, as the law demands.'

Claude blinked furiously. 'Aye well, I can't see me going that far, George. Eggs, bacon, fried bread and a plate of porridge is about as far as I'll go for far as the service of victuals is concerned. But I might include an orange juice or grapefruit ...'

'So long as you buy them from me, Claude.'

'That would depend on your price, George.'

I smiled at the banter which was going on and began to appreciate the firm demarcation lines which were drawn in the case of any local business. George was not going to allow Claude to poach any of his potential customers. But if that couple from Wolverhampton had seen fit to remain with Claude for several days, then his hosting abilities and his standard of accommodation might be better than expected.

When our meal arrived, Mary and I concentrated upon enjoying it; we bought

Claude and his cronies a drink in return and before we departed for home, I wished Claude all the best in his enterprise and reminded him to be on his guard against confidence tricksters bearing accents, in smart clothes and sporting big wallets.

It was the following Saturday morning when there was an almighty clattering on my office door. I was off duty, hoping for a relaxed and enjoyable weekend with my young family, and was reading the morning papers over a cup of coffee. As always in such cases, Mary went to answer the knock—she was quite an expert at diverting to Ashfordly Police Station those with non-urgent business who called in my off-duty time or referring them to one of the neighbouring rural beat officers who was covering the area in my absence. In a genuine emergency, of course, I would respond and I soon realized that, in this case, she had decided it was an emergency.

It was Claude Jeremiah Greengrass. He followed her into the house with a look of anguish on his whiskery features.

'Claude!' I got to my feet to receive him. 'What's happened?'

'I'll tell you what's happened!' he cried.

'I've been diddled, that's what's happened. Conned. Deprived of my rightful dues!'

'You'd better sit down.' I waved him towards the settee while Mary went off to fetch him a coffee. He sat on the edge, wringing his hands and looking a picture of abject misery. 'So, what exactly has happened?'

'Them folks you sent me.' His eyes stared into mine as if it was all my fault. 'Them customers. They've gone, that's what. Without paying. And they've taken a dozen new-laid eggs and two brace of rabbits ... and paid not a penny, Constable. I call that highway robbery!'

'I did warn you, Claude.' I hoped I did not sound as if I was crowing over his dilemma. 'I warned you and George about confidence tricksters who leave without paying ... so how much do they owe?'

'Well, I mean, bed and breakfast for seven nights at a pound each, that's fourteen pounds. Four rabbits—five bob each. Another quid. And a dozen eggs. Three and six.'

'Fifteen pounds, three and sixpence,' I said. 'And you would have a register for them to sign upon arrival, I take it? With their name and address? I said you'd need one.'

'Well, no, I mean, I never thought it was really necessary, not when I was in the business in such a small way ...'

'Claude, I told you that if you are in the hotel business ...'

'Hotel?' he cried. 'It's not an hotel, it's my second-best bedroom!'

'But you are taking in people for reward, sleeping there for one night or more. That means you must keep a register. The rules apply to any premises where lodging or sleeping accommodation is provided for reward—you should obtain their names, addresses and nationalities, and retain the records for at least one year.'

'Aye, well, I didn't, did I?'

'And now you expect us to chase those unknown people to an unknown destination and have them prosecuted for failing to pay you for illegal accommodation—and thus generating publicity that might create some interest by the tax man ...'

'But, well, Constable, it's not right, is it? Folks breaking the law and getting away with it!'

'It's not right at all, Claude. So you, as an upstanding citizen and man of principle, what would you wish me to do? Report this and go through all the procedures, or let you send the couple a bill first?'

'But I told you, I don't know who they are.'

'Did you note their car number?'

'No, why should I do that? They were decent folk, like me.'

'Well, if you didn't note it, I did, that day they asked me about your facilities. I'll try and trace them through the motor taxation department at County Hall. And I might be able to have them prosecuted for obtaining credit by fraud—but it would mean you'd have to come to court as a witness for the prosecution.'

'Witness for the prosecution? Me? You must be joking! I'm not a grass! I just want you to do summat ...'

'Well, I can't proceed without an official complaint and a statement from you, then, when we catch them, you'll have to appear in court in due course, to tell the magistrates what happened.'

'But them folks are kindred spirits of mine, Constable. Friends, even. We was right friendly, getting real close we were. First-name terms and all that. So I can't take them to court ... I can't grass on my own kind ... can I?'

'They've done you out of your money, Claude, don't forget. Fine friends they turned out to be! But I'll tell you what; I'll try and find out who they are from their car registration number. I can't do that until Monday anyway. When I get their details, I'll give them to you, and you can send them a bill. If they pay up, you won't have to go to court.'

'And if they don't?'

'That's when I'll want you to become a witness for the prosecution, to make your official complaint about the offence you allege they have committed.'

'I'll have to think about that,' he grunted. 'So are you going to circulate details about them? To warn others not to get taken in like me?'

'If you make an official complaint, Claude, yes.'

'All this officialdom isn't the sort of thing I go for.' He was most reluctant to get involved in anything which hinted at a court action. 'Can I think it over?'

'Do that,' I suggested, and off he went.

On the following Monday morning, I rang the motor taxation department of the County Borough of Wolverhampton which was then based in the town hall at Bilston in Staffordshire. As the registration number began with the letters AJW, I knew the vehicle would be recorded with that department, even if the owner of the car lived outside their area—but it wasn't listed. The number on the old Ford was a false one—it had not been issued. My heart sank. On the day the couple had spoken to me, I had not checked the car; they had been villains on my patch, I had failed to recognize them as such and now Claude had suffered.

I went to see him. I told him I could not trace the couple who had swindled him because they were riding around in a car bearing false number plates and he seemed relieved.

'I'm not going to prosecute,' he told me. 'And I shan't get you to try and find them, Constable. I don't want to get myself tangled up with the law or courts or prosecutions or owt like that. It's all too much hassle for an old chap like me. Anyroad, that'll please you. And I'm not going to do any more bed-and-breakfasting so that'll please George. And so everybody's happy and I'm a few quid out of pocket after learning a hard lesson.'

But I was far from happy at my own handling of the affair. I'd let a couple of villains slip through my fingers and so I decided to circulate all police forces a description of the car and its occupants. When Sergeant Blaketon questioned the reason for my decision, I told him—he chuckled at Claude's dilemma, but did agree that every effort should be made to trace this second team of confidence tricksters.

But, like the handsome couple who'd tricked their way through our area before them, they were never found.

Later, Claude told me that if they did return, he had a special egg surprise awaiting them—he'd bombard them with all the bad eggs he collected from now until the day of their arrival. I advised him to wait until I was overseas on holiday before he took that kind of drastic action. I wanted to know nothing about it.

'It will not be legal, it's an assault,' I warned him.

'I'll make sure you never know about it,' he muttered. 'But it's a sad thing when a chap has to take the law into his own hands.'

I had to agree.

If Claude Jeremiah Greengrass thought he led a hard life and that others had an easier means of earning their livelihood, then Medwin Isaacs thought that life in the countryside was absolute bliss. For him, a townie by birth and a townie by inclination, the countryside provided a place of solitude and silence; for Medwin, it offered a refreshing change from the hurly-burly, noise and constant presence of traffic and active people, all unwelcome aspects of his daily life in the city.

His home was a modest terraced house without a garden and it was in the centre of York, not far from Clifford's Tower. Medwin worked in the city's offices of British Railways. His job was to purchase equipment and stationery for the multitude of clerks who occupied the multitude of offices which were used to keep the nationalized rail services running on time.

Some said he did a poor job because the trains were invariably late and when they did arrive, they were filthy but Medwin did not know that. He never used the trains, except on those rare occasions when he could usefully benefit from his concessionary tickets. The moment he finished work on a Friday evening, after a week of persuading the staff they could last a little longer with their present equipment, or borrow an envelope from a colleague or that their ballpoint still had a few days' worth of ink left in it, he and his wife would pack their Mini-car and head for the North York Moors.

Unable or unwilling to afford the finest hotels, they rented a modest variety of tiny country cottages and seemed able to select those which were tucked away at the end of a disused lane or located on the lonesome heights of a stretch of inhospitable moorland. They managed to find the most lonely of places, often discovering cottages without running water or electricity which explained their modest rental. But the more isolated and rustic the cottage, the more they seemed to like it. Such bleak places were Medwin's idea of absolute bliss.

Once inside their chosen weekend home, Medwin and Bethany seldom ventured out—they were not keen on natural history, they did not watch birds or study plants, they did not paint or take photographs, ramble along the highways and byways or visit rural pubs to sample their beer or bar meals. In fact, no one really knew what they did once they arrived because they would light a fire, put on the radio or take out a book, and do very little else, apart from those moments when Mrs Isaacs cooked a modest meal by using the ingredients she had brought.

I knew all this because people talked about Mr and Mrs Isaacs—invariably, the cottages they rented belonged to the local farmers. In the past, they had been used by agricultural workers but when the Isaacs arrived, they were not too welcome—the farmers knew they'd never sell them eggs or milk because they brought their own city-purchased supplies. In fact, they never bought anything in the village shop—no newspapers, supplies of any kind, food or groceries. No good wholesome country food was ever purchased and they made no contribution to the village economy. They simply drove to their cottage, closed the doors and remained there until late on the Sunday evening when they drove back to York so that Medwin could return to work on Monday morning.

That somewhat unrealistic existence appeared to be their idea of country life. I knew something about them because the sister of a friend of mine worked in the same offices as Medwin and she often talked about his quaint ways. At work, it seems he was a little Hitler, ruling his precious kingdom with an iron hand and not allowing the office staff to acquire new envelopes, reams of paper, pencils, blotting paper or even paper clips unless he was satisfied they had truly exhausted their previous allocation.

One could only imagine his mental anguish upon receiving a requisition for something as expensive as a new typewriter or office chair; he delayed such issues for months on end, wondering whether British Railways could afford such luxuries for its menial staff. It seems he did not favour office tea swindles either, preferring to work at his desk without a tea or coffee break or a ten-minute rest from his arduous task.

On top of all that, he disliked hilarity in the workplace. In truth, British Railways had a wonderful servant in Medwin—on the face of it, it seemed he saved them a fortune by preventing waste by the staff, but in fact his stockroom cupboards were always full of out-of-date stationery which he had never issued. That was his idea of saving money—and he always wrote on both sides of scrap paper. There were times I wondered if he was in charge of buying new railway engines or carriages because the existing ones did not seem to be the best—they seemed to be very old ones which were being run until they conked out somewhere between King's Cross and Edinburgh. And if you saw some of the brushes and mops used by the carriage cleaning staff you'd think they'd been used since the beginning of the railways ... there is no doubt that the Medwin mentality did, I believe, infiltrate British Railways to a remarkable depth. Britain's taxpayers would have no idea how much the Medwins of this world were striving to reduce their contribution to the costs of running British Railways.

My first meeting with Medwin came one Sunday morning in September. It was a cool but sunny morning and I had just returned from Mass. He arrived on my doorstep about ten o'clock when I was still dressed in civilian clothes.

At that time, I had never met him, consequently I did not immediately realize that the little flat-capped gentleman with the black moustache and round spectacles was Medwin.

'Good morning,' I smiled as I opened the door to him.

'You are the constable?' He looked me up and down, his hard grey eyes scrutinizing my mode of attire.

'PC Rhea,' I said. 'I'm not on duty just yet, that's why I am wearing civilian clothes.'

'Ah, the luxuries of country life!' He attempted a smile. 'Perhaps I should not trouble you, Constable. I can return when it is more convenient.'

'No,' I said. 'If you've come far, I'm sure I can either help you or ask a duty officer to come and visit you. So, what's the problem?'

'Noise,' he said. 'I wish to lodge a complaint about excessive noise.'

'This morning?' I asked. 'Is it troublesome at this moment?'

'It is,' he nodded gravely. 'Very troublesome, if I may say so.'

'Then tell me where it is,' I invited him.

'Those fields across the dale.' He pointed somewhere in the wide beyond. 'Motor cycles, dozens of them. Roaring about the place.'

'Ah.' I knew the place. 'It's an approved track. They're scrambles riders ...'

'Scrambles?' He frowned, puzzled at my expression.

'Cross-country motor cycling,' I tried to explain. 'Young lads with specially adapted bikes race around a rough, muddy, stone-ridden course. It takes tremendous skill and courage. They use a track on land at Hawthorn Grange, it's out of the way and well off the beaten track about two miles from here. The farm has lots of scrubland, sir, and no one objects to the lads using it for their scrambling—both in practice and in competition. At this time of day, I expect they'll be practising for a series of races later this afternoon.'

'But it is so intrusive, Constable. I wish to lodge a formal complaint under the Noise Abatement Act.'

'The Noise Abatement Act does not apply to that kind of noise nuisance,' I advised him. 'You'll have to contact the local authority, at the council offices. They deal with such things. They will serve a notice on the organizers or someone responsible, ordering them to abate the nuisance—that's if they are satisfied there are genuine grounds for complaint. It is not a police matter.'

'Really? I thought country policemen dealt with everything that was unlawful?'

'Not quite,' I said. 'There are lots of nuisances and civil laws which are not within the province of the police service. I'm sorry I cannot be more helpful but I shall be visiting the scramble meeting later in the day. I will mention your complaint to the organizer.'

'Thank you, Constable. Now, you will need my name—I am Medwin Isaacs,' and he gave me his address, adding he was staying at Stable Cottage which was in High Garth Lane above Aidensfield. And off he went.

I had no intention of registering this grumble as an official complaint for I had done my duty by referring Medwin to the local authority. I doubt if he would succeed in having the noise levels reduced—when the use of the land had been suggested as a possible site for scrambles meetings, the problem of noise had been one of the considerations and, in spite of a few objections at the time, the proposal had been approved.

As the site was on my beat, I was very aware of any potential problems which might be created and for that reason, always kept in close touch with the organizers of the meetings. But the scrambles course was very remote and the noise little more than the buzzing of a hive of bees.

It was known, of course, that the people who objected most vehemently were those who came to live in the village from elsewhere. The long-term residents did not complain—and we'd had incomers complain about the smell of pig farms, the noise of bird scarers, smoke from bonfires, the movement of farm machinery in the early hours of the morning, the sound of milking parlours, grain driers and more. It was amazing how many townies came to live in the countryside and promptly began to grumble about ordinary rural activities. And Medwin Isaacs seemed such a fellow.

It was during that time that Middle Mires Cottage was put on the market. It was a remarkable place, a very old stone-built house of beautiful proportions if rather on the small side with limited accommodation. It was sited in the middle of a small garden surrounded by a dry stone wall. Totally unmodernized, it had no running water, electricity, mains drainage or inside toilet; the loo was a small stone shed in one corner of the garden while a lean-to shelter offered cover for a small motor car, motor bike or a wheelbarrow beside the house. Furthermore, there was no road to the house. Access was via an unmade lane which twisted and turned between two high hedges before emerging into a large open field. Middle Mires Cottage was in the middle of that field, and the rough track led across the grass to the cottage gate.

It was about a mile and a half from the nearest part of Aidensfield, that being a dutch barn belonging to High Mires Farm, and the name of the house gave a clue to its past. That field had once been marshy ground in the dale below High Mires, hence the name of Middle Mire. Years ago, the marsh had been drained to form the present field and although it was low-lying and not far from the stream which flowed along the foot of the dale, it was not subjected to flooding. The field was now cultivated and variously used as a meadow, grazing ground and for growing wheat or barley. Currently, it sported a healthy crop of ripening wheat.

But Medwin and Bethany noticed the 'For Sale' sign, went to inspect the premises and immediately fell in love with it. This was their dream cottage—small, isolated, rustic, uncluttered with harmful modern innovations, surrounded by nothing but fields and nature and deep in the North Yorkshire countryside. Being prudent people, they had substantial savings and, wishing to fulfil their lifelong dream of living in a rustic idyll, they bought it. I discovered that the village had some newcomers when I was in Joe Steel's shop-cum-post office one Monday morning.

'I see Herbert Bainbridge of High Mires has got rid of that old cottage of his,' Joe remarked during our chat about village matters.

'Knocked it down, you mean?' I could not see the place had any modern com-mercial value.

'No, some idiot from the town has bought it. Some folks'll buy anything,' he grinned. 'Herbert was thinking of gutting it and using it as a barn or something similar, but decided he'd cash in on the craze for buying country cottages.'

'A wise man!' I grinned.

'A good move because, bingo—it was snapped up by this townie.'

'So who are our new pseudo-villagers?' I asked.

'A funny little chap called Isaacs and his wife. Medwin and Bethany. He works for British Railways in York. He won't last long—one good winter will see him off! We've found that's the finest means of reminding townies that the countryside is not suburbia with smells—a thumping good blizzard or two works wonders and sends 'em all rushing back home.'

'He called to see me a few weeks ago,' I recalled. 'Grumbling about the noise of scramble bikes.'

'Oh, crumbs! He's not a grumbler, is he?' Joe frowned. 'We can do without incoming grumblers.'

'I fear he might be!' I warned him, knowing he would spread the word among the other villagers if Medwin proved to be a persistent complainer. And he did turn out to be one—and the person at the rough end of most of Medwin's grouses was Farmer Herbert Bainbridge, the man who'd sold him the cottage. There being no telephone at the cottage, Medwin had arrived at the farm kitchen door shortly after eight one morning to register his first complaint.

'I wish to make a complaint,' he said to Mrs Bainbridge as she confronted him.

'What about?' she asked.

'The noise,' chirped Medwin. 'Shooting noises.'

'It's bird scarers,' she smiled. 'They're automatic bird scarers; they're timed to go off every few minutes and sound like gunshots. They scare the birds off our crops, Mr Isaacs, and off our neighbours' crops. We all use them.'

'But I did not come here to listen to the constant sound of shooting! It started first thing this morning ...'

'They begin at dawn when the birds wake and begin to feed. This is the countryside, Mr Isaacs.' Jessie Bainbridge was a friendly woman. 'You'll soon get accustomed to such things and in a very short time, you won't even notice the noises.'

'I notice all noises, Mrs Bainbridge. I think I shall have to write to the council about this, and get something done.'

'You do that,' she smiled sweetly at him. 'Yes, you do that, Mr Isaacs.'

Medwin's next grumble came when the Bainbridges began to harvest their corn. The combines began work the moment the grain was sufficiently dry and they worked late into the night, the monotonous roar of their machinery rumbling long and loud in the darkness. Several worked in tandem and the rumble and roar of their movement echoed in the still of the early September evening. It was this which compelled Medwin to knock on Mrs Bainbridge's door at ten o'clock one evening.

'Mrs Bainbridge, I have to rise early to drive to York for work and I need to be guaranteed a good night's sleep, yet here I am listening to the constant roar of that thing in the fields.'

'A combine harvester, Mr Isaacs.'

'But do you have to cut the stuff at this time of night? Don't you people ever sleep?'

'We work when there's work to be done, Mr Isaacs. As a country lover, I thought you would realize that. There's no union rules here, you know, no office routine, no set hours or overtime or timed meal breaks. We work until we finish and there's no way you and your townie ideas will change that!'

'Then I shall write to the council and register a formal complaint,' he muttered, stomping away—and she just smiled. She'd tell Herbert about this visit when he finished for the night.

It was inevitable that I learned of Medwin's grumbling; his non-stop nattering soon became the talk of Aidensfield where his constant grouse was about noise in the countryside. Poor Herbert Bainbridge and his wife were the most long-suffering because Medwin complained about cockerels crowing at dawn, cows mooing in the early morning as they ambled in to be milked, hens cackling when they laid eggs, tractors chugging, combines roaring and corn driers humming. He even had the audacity to comment about the noise of rooks cawing in the trees at High Mires Farm and of the metallic sounds which emanated from the farrier's shop as the farrier fashioned horseshoes for some of the local riding stables and horse-racing establishments.

Now that Medwin was living permanently in the countryside, the occasional noise which had hitherto disturbed him only at weekends was now a permanent fixture of his new world.

We realized that things hadn't worked out for Medwin when he and Bethany went off to York for a quiet weekend in a cottage they rented near the railway station and when they did likewise on several successive occasions, it was clear that he regarded the town as the ideal place to spend a quiet, relaxed weekend.

We knew what would happen next. He would put Middle Mires Cottage on the market. And sure enough, it wasn't long before a 'For Sale' notice appeared at the gate. We all thought it would never sell—not many people were daft enough to buy that remote, unmodernized cottage in the middle of a field. It was for sale for several weeks but eventually the sign did come down. Someone had bought the house. That was the surprise for us all and we wondered if another dreaming townsperson had bought it—but it did mean that Medwin returned to the solitude, anonymity and loneliness of city life to leave us all in peace.

A few weeks later, I visited Herbert Bainbridge at High Mires Farm for a routine inspection of his livestock registers. His paperwork was always up to date and accurate, and I had no qualms in appending my signature to confirm my visit. As always, Jessie invited me to stay for a cup of coffee and a piece of gingerbread and cheese; happily, I consented. As we chatted, I recalled Medwin's brief occupancy of Middle Mires Cottage and commented, 'I see Medwin Isaacs managed to sell the cottage. Any idea who bought it?'

Herbert grinned wickedly.

'Aye, me. I bought it back from him.'

'You did?' I was surprised.

'He lost more than a few quid, I might add,' chuckled Herbert. 'I thought I'd teach him not to come here and start complaining about country ways, so when I realized he'd never sell the spot, I offered him a daft price. He was that keen to get back to York he accepted. So I've got my cottage back and I hope that daft Medwin and his missus have learned a lesson. It's been a costly one for them, I'd say,' he mused.

'I doubt if they have learned a lesson,' I had to say. 'People like Medwin never learn from their experience—they'll always blame others for their problems. But what are you going to do with the cottage?'

'Let it off to holiday-makers,' he smiled. 'There's a demand for old, primitive cottages—only for short-term visits, mind! Folks like to think they're camping in the fields. I'll be advertising in the papers for next year, Nick, so if you hear of anybody who wants a nice quiet place in the countryside, tell 'em about Middle Mires Cottage.'

'I will,' I promised, but made a mental note not to mention noisy combines, tractors, cockerels and the other sounds of the Yorkshire countryside at work.

6 The Silver Hawk

The wild hawk stood with the down on
  his beak,
And stared, with his foot on the prey.
    Alfred, Lord Tennyson (1809–1892)

It takes a good deal of imagination to
calculate how the arrival of a spectacular
but rare bird of prey could help to solve a
puzzling series of petty crimes—but by a
string of linked coincidences, that's exactly
what happened one summer on the moors
above Aidensfield.

It was a hot and cloudless Monday in
June when I received a telephone call from
Tom Maxfield who farmed at High Ghyll
Hall. It was about four in the afternoon
when he rang me and by chance I was
working in the office attached to my
house, typing a report for the coroner
about a recent sudden death. A call from
High Ghyll Hall was unusual because
it was one of the most remote of the
farms on my beat, well and truly off

the proverbial beaten track but enjoying the most beautiful locations with stunning views to the south across the moors. But Tom did not want to explain the reason for his call, not over the telephone. The confidentiality of telephone calls was something that seemed to worry a lot of country people. Tom asked me to pop in when I was passing, and I said I would be on patrol later that same evening and would drive out to visit him.

But the splendidly situated High Ghyll Hall wasn't the sort of place anyone popped into while passing!

The magnificent stone house, known locally as a hall as were many of the larger farmhouses of this region, occupied a sheltered and isolated position at the head of its own small dale. That was Ghylldale which led deep into the moors above Aidensfield. The farm, with mixed arable land, moorland sheep and beef cattle, was set in acres of wild moorland and accessible only by a long, gated track which twisted and turned for almost two miles along the side of the dale; the track, which passed one or two lonely cottages *en route*, did not lead to any other place, consequently High Ghyll Hall was not the sort of place you passed *en route* to anywhere else. Tom, however, had no real appreciation of its isolation because he made regular trips into Aidensfield and beyond to Ashfordly, Eltering and Harrowby markets. Such journeys were quite normal for him—he'd lived there all his life, having inherited the farm from his father.

For the rest of us, a visit to this remote spot was not something anyone did casually—it required a determined effort, the opening of six five-bar gates and some uncomfortable bumping along an unmade track before arriving at the farm. Those of us who knew the district always made a phone call to Tom and Margaret Maxfield before setting out from Aidensfield, just to make sure they were at home. It was a long way there and back for nowt!

Pondering the reason for Tom's phone call, I arrived at the farm at 6.30 that same evening to find Tom and Margaret settling down for their evening meal, which they called tea, and, as was the custom hereabouts, I was invited to join them at the table.

A sturdy jovial man in his late fifties, Tom had a round red face and thin fair hair which looked like straw; with hands like shovels and feet like even bigger shovels, he stood some six feet six inches tall in his heavy working shirt and corduroy trousers. Margaret, his wife, was just as tiny, a little sparrow of a woman with sharp features, darting grey eyes and thin legs. She played an equal part in the running of his family business. Locally, she was regarded as an expert on Friesian cattle and was a regular prize-winner with her animals at Yorkshire agricultural shows.

'Come in, Mr Rhea,' she invited as I arrived at the kitchen door.

'Sit down there, Mr Rhea,' commanded Tom, pointing to a beautiful carver chair at the head of the kitchen table which was set for a meal. 'Then we can talk.'

I obeyed and was next presented with a feast of smoked ham, home-grown tomatoes, lettuce, cucumber, cold new potatoes and soft tiny carrots, to be followed by a whopping slice of gooseberry pie and custard, all washed down with a mug of milky tea. A light meal for them—a feast for me.

'Now then, Mr Rhea.' Tom waited until I was settled before my overflowing plate before he mentioned the reason for his call. 'It's good of you to turn out like this. You'll be wondering why I called you in?'

'Yes, it's not often I get summoned to these parts,' I smiled.

'Aye, well, I didn't like to say owt on t'telephone, you never know who's listening in.'

I wondered how he perceived the telephone, but was growing more interested now as I tucked into my meal, wondering if a drama was about to be unfolded.

'Confidential, is it?' I asked.

'Nay, not in so many words, but I don't like conducting my personal business on t'telephone. What it is, Mr Rhea, is we've had some money pinched. And food. Ham and stuff. Tomatoes, eggs. At least, we think we have.'

'They could have had the food if only they'd asked,' Margaret added. 'There's always food to spare, folks just have to ask.'

'You said you think you've had some stolen?' I wondered who on earth would steal from this lonely place. 'Aren't you sure?'

'Well, it was my egg money,' Margaret explained. 'I keep it in that drawer over

235

there,' and she pointed to a sideboard with drawers at the far side of the huge kitchen. 'To be honest, Mr Rhea, I never know exactly how much there is in there, and we do dip into it for spending in the village—groceries, stamps, hen food, a drop of petrol or diesel now and again, and so on. But I'm sure summat like five pounds has gone, in coins, and I know Tom hasn't taken it.'

'Never laid a finger on it,' he grinned. 'It's her money, you see, Mr Rhea. More than my life's worth to snaffle a bob or two.'

'And you never lock your door?'

'I shouldn't think that kitchen door's been locked for nigh on two hundred years, Mr Rhea, give or take a month or two. There's no need to up here, is there?'

'Not until now,' I had to say, following with, 'And do you employ anyone? Has anyone been working here lately?'

'Only Aud Harry Fenton from down the lane, but he's not been in all week, he's got rheumatics. But he's been with us ever since he was a lad, Mr Rhea, whenever that was—in my father's time, I should think, or my grandfather's. He's allus been an aud feller while I've known him. He must be getting on for eighty and can still do a full day's hay-timing. But he'd not take owt without asking, not even an apple or a tatie.'

'So when did the money disappear?' was my next question.

'It's hard to say, Mr Rhea,' Margaret frowned. 'I'd say yesterday afternoon, Sunday mebbe, or even Saturday sometime. Both days, Tom was down the fields but yesterday I went into Aidensfield to see my sister. The kitchen would be empty from after Sunday dinner till just before teatime.'

'And has anything else been stolen? You have shotguns in the house, I'm sure, and a .22 rifle. All farmers have them.'

'I checked, Mr Rhea, none of the guns were touched, nor the ammo. No, it's just as we said, food and a bit o' cash.'

'And did you see anyone on the road when you went into the village? Strange cars? Cyclists? Hikers?'

She shook her head. 'Sorry, no, never saw a soul.'

In such circumstances, especially when the facts are rather uncertain, it is always difficult to be sure that a crime has been committed—there was no break-in, the losers weren't absolutely sure if anything had been taken and even if it had, they did not know how much was missing.

In such a lonely situation, casual callers were unlikely, as were travelling thieves or opportunist villains. I looked at the drawer concerned—it contained various items of cutlery but in the front there was a money box with a slit in the lid—Margaret always popped her egg money in there and used it for small expenditure. She could never say precisely how much it contained at any one time, only knowing instinctively that when she opened the tin today, there was less than she'd expected. It now contained 18s. 6d. in coins, when she'd expected something like £10 or £12. Similarly, the pantry contained shelves and trays of food and vegetables, and all she could say was that several slices of ham appeared to have gone, along with a pocketful of tomatoes and half a dozen fresh eggs. I knew she was not imagining this but even so, due to the lack of precise information, I knew that Sergeant Blaketon would not allow the losses to be regarded as a crime. I therefore decided not to record this event as a crime but told the Maxfields I would bear it in mind during my forthcoming patrols. I promised to keep an eye open for any likely suspects in the area, and asked them in return to let me know if more food or money disappeared. During my return journey to Aidensfield, I called at the cottages and farms along the lane to ask if any strangers had been noticed, but none had. That tended to support the official attitude that Margaret had made a mistake and had miscalculated the contents of her tin and pantry shelf.

But more money did vanish, although not from High Ghyll Hall. The next report came from Nab Side Farm, Briggsby, the home of John and Frances Broadley.

In their mid-thirties, this young couple had rented the farm from Ashfordly Estate about three years earlier and were creating a fine milking herd of Jerseys. They rang me the following morning, Tuesday, with a story that bore remarkable similarities to that of Tom and Margaret Maxfield. Yesterday afternoon, someone had sneaked into the farmhouse, entered John's office and stolen £10 in mixed silver and notes from his petty cash box. Half a pound of bacon rashers, a string of sausages and two pork chops had also disappeared from the

239

cool shelf of the pantry.

There had been no break-in, entry to the house being via the kitchen door which had been closed but not locked as the couple were working in the milking parlour. But John and Frances were not in doubt about their loss—John maintained a good accounting system and could trace every penny he spent. As with the Maxfields, I asked whether their guns had been stolen, but they had not, the only missing items being the money and some food.

In many ways, Nab Side Farm emulated High Ghyll in that it was an isolated farmstead on the moors although in this case the house was perched on the side of a hill, known locally as Briggsby Nab. A single track led to Nab Side from Briggsby but in this instance continued beyond it to serve several farms and houses before continuing around the head of the dale and returning to Briggsby via the far side of the valley. There was no direct road link between High Ghyll and Nab Side, a trek from one farm to the other requiring a trip of some five miles if one went by road—but an examination of the map told me the farms were in fact less than half a mile apart, albeit separated by the imposing bulk of the heather-covered Briggsby Nab.

As I prepared to drive out to interview John and Francis Broadley, it occurred to me that the thief or thieves must be on foot, a hiker perhaps, someone who was tramping across the wilderness in that desolate part of my beat. Or perhaps camping? Otherwise why steal food? On my way to Nab End, I decided to visit Aidensfield shop-cum-post office to see if any strangers had called to spend money, but Joe Steel, the shopkeeper, shook his head. I told him about the two raids on isolated farms and he promised to let me know if he noticed any likely culprits, especially those who might be spending money in his shop. It was while I was in the shop that Daniel Ellis entered. A self-employed carpenter clad in his brown overall, he looked harassed and worried but seemed relieved at my presence.

'Nick, just the chap! I heard you were in here,' he breathed, looking at me and then at Joe Steel. 'Have either of you seen our Simon?'

'No.' I shook my head, and Joe did likewise. 'Why?' I asked.

'He's not at school,' he sighed heavily.

'Playing truant! I never would have thought that of my lad!'

'Truant?' I knew Simon Ellis. He was a pleasant boy who was regularly seen riding his bike about the village, sometimes visiting his grandparents, sometimes playing on the cricket field or simply wandering about the countryside looking for wild animals and birds.

'He's not the sort to skip school,' Dan said. 'He likes it, he likes his teacher and he's not being bullied. It was his teacher, Josie Preston, who told me, she rang this morning ...'

'Is it the first time?' I asked.

'So far as I know,' Dan confirmed. 'She said nowt about him bunking off on Friday or any other day.'

'Where was he at the weekend, Dan?' I was thinking of those raids at the farms.

'At home, playing around the village, riding his bike, popping to see his grandparents, going for walks by the river or biking up to the moors looking for birds, that sort of thing. Doing all the things young lads do in the countryside.'

'And this morning? Did he let you think he was going to school as normal?'

'Aye, he set off on his bike just after half

eight as usual, bright as a button, just like he allus does.'

'So where do you think he might have gone?' I was anxious not to spark off a massive hunt for the boy if he was simply hiding somewhere in the village but, simultaneously, I had to bear in mind the possibility he might be in trouble, or that he could get lost and injure himself.

'He could be anywhere, Nick,' he said. 'Mind you, he's allus gone off by himself, he's used to roaming about the countryside, he'll not be taking harm, if that's what you're thinking.'

I established from Dan, a good-looking, dark-haired man in his early forties, that Simon was ten years old, about four feet tall with dark-brown hair, a freckled complexion and brown eyes. When he'd left home this morning, he was wearing a white shirt with short sleeves, a pair of grey short trousers, grey socks and black shoes.

He carried his satchel of brown leather which contained an apple and an orange along with some books. He'd get his dinner at school. He had a bike, a boy's Raleigh which was blue with a white seat and white handbar grips. Dan told me that none of

243

his other clothes were missing, the only additional thing he'd taken being a pair of binoculars given to him as a birthday present by his grandfather.

'Why take the binoculars to school?' I asked.

'He's looking for a silver hawk,' said Dan. 'A few weeks ago, his grandad told him the legend of the silver hawk and since then, the lad's been looking for it. He reckons he spotted it on the moors near Witch Hill, a big white bird he said, but I told him it would be a seagull. Anyroad, he took his binoculars to school this morning and said he would look for the silver hawk after school, before he came home for his tea.'

'Legend of the silver hawk?' I asked. 'I've never heard of that!'

'It's hardly ever mentioned these days, but my dad likes to tell the tale. They say a silver hawk used to live around Witch Hill, centuries ago that was, when folks believed in witches. Witches were said to make cattle sick, turn milk sour, prevent hens and geese from laying eggs, stop the harvest ripening, that sort of thing. But the silver hawk, being a white bird, was the symbol of good, something the witches

244

hated, and so long as the silver hawk was around, the witches couldn't operate their wicked spells. So a silver hawk on the moors was a sign of good fortune for the farmers and country folk hereabout and therefore for the whole village—hens and geese would lay well, cows would thrive and so on.'

'And so your dad has told Simon all about it and you think he's gone up to Witch Hill already, instead of waiting until school's finished?' I suggested. 'Armed with his bike, his apple and orange, and a pair of binoculars? It's quite a way for a lad—two or three miles at least!'

'It is, but he often goes up there; we never worry about him, he's quite sensible—and he was up there over the weekend,' Dan admitted. 'When we quizzed him on Saturday afternoon, he said he'd been watching the silver hawk flying over Aidensfield Moor. I know nowt about birds and reckon he's been seeing a big seagull. But yes, I think he could have gone up there instead of going to school.'

'You've been to look?' I asked.

'Not yet, that was my next job after checking around the village.'

'Right,' I said. 'If you go up to Witch Hill, I'll check the area around Briggsby Nab. I've got to call at Nab Side Farm this morning—my next job in fact—so I'll keep my eyes and ears open. Then I'll come back and see you later, say lunchtime, to see if there's any progress?'

'Aye, right,' he agreed.

I did not explain my reason for travelling out to Nab Side Farm because I did not want Dan to think his son was under suspicion as a petty thief—but I knew I would have to interview Simon about the thefts when he returned home. I did not regard this as a missing child drama—not yet anyway. It was just a case of truancy at this stage, but decided I should call at the school before heading into the hills.

Josie Preston, Simon's teacher, greeted me and when I explained that I'd been talking to Simon's dad, she smiled.

'I had to tell him, but forgot to mention Friday.'

'He played truant on Friday too?' I asked.

'Yes, at first when he didn't come for assembly, I thought he was ill and left it at that. Then later in the morning one of the children said they'd seen Simon on his bike, heading out of the village when he should have been coming to school. I rang the family home straight away, but Mr Ellis was out on a job, I think; there was no reply. Mrs Ellis always goes to the market on Fridays, on the early bus, so I missed her and couldn't contact either of them. By the time the Ellises returned, school was over and anyway, I saw Simon heading homewards on his bike. He was too far off for me to catch him for a chat, but I knew he was safe. Because I got no reply from the house, I think he was absent from home all day Friday, returning in time for his tea, just as if he'd been to school.'

'That makes sense. You know about the silver hawk legend?' I asked her.

'Yes, I do. And he did tell me he'd seen a silver hawk one day after school, but said I was not to tell anyone about it! It was a secret, he said, only his dad and mum knew. I have no idea what he saw, to be honest. I did wonder if he'd imagined the whole thing.'

'I think that's where he's gone this morning,' I said. 'Somewhere on those moors looking for his silver hawk. But there is no such bird, his dad thinks he's been watching a seagull, probably a herring gull if it was a large whitish bird.'

I told Josie I was on my way to Briggsby Nab and that Simon's father was heading towards the Witch Hill area, so between us we should locate the truant boy. I was content in my assessment of the situation, ie. that I did not need to be panicked into arranging a full-scale search, and I arrived at Nab Side Farm without a hitch.

Over coffee and fruit cake, I settled down as John and Francis showed me the scene of their crime. Sometime yesterday afternoon, their house had been entered via the closed but unlocked door. The thief or thieves had explored the house because several drawers had been searched and left open but nothing taken other than cash from John's office and some food from the pantry. I asked the usual questions about suspicious persons in the vicinity, people working on the farm, people with legitimate access to the house who might have been tempted, but came down firmly in the belief that the thief was someone who was camping or living rough in the area. Judging by the locations of both attacked premises, the villain or villains were able to watch for the departure of the householders. It would be a simple matter to conceal oneself on the moors and carry out a scrutiny of the premises from the slopes of Briggsby Nab—especially through a good pair of binoculars—and then enter when the occupants had left. But would a ten-year-old boy do that?

Questions from John and Francis failed to elicit any useful information about likely suspects and so I left their house, promising that I would keep them informed about any developments. And like yesterday, I called at various farms and houses between Nab Side and Briggsby—and this time, I was in luck.

I noticed Ted Wilkinson, a retired garage mechanic, weeding his borders at Bilberry Cottage half a mile or so beyond the entrance to Nab Side and stopped for a chat. When I asked about strangers using the road, he said, 'I only saw a lad on a bike, a young lad. I remember thinking he should be at school but he looked smart and tidy. That would be ten o'clockish, when I was taking my dog out.'

'Where was he?' I asked.

'Well, he put his bike behind a wall, up near Larch Gill, that's at the bottom of Witch Hill. It's a blue bike with a white seat. Then I saw him climbing up the moor from there, using that dried-up bed of the beck as a footpath.'

'Thanks,' I breathed a sigh of relief. 'But did he go anywhere near Nab Side Farm?'

'No, nowhere, Mr Rhea. It's just that I thought it odd, him not being at school.'

'Thanks Ted, I'll see if I can trace him.'

I found Simon's bike within half an hour. He had taken it through a gate and rested it against a high dry stone wall so that it was invisible to anyone driving past. And ahead, I saw the rocky bed of the dried-up beck or gill as such small streams are known on these moors. The gill flowed from the heights of the moor to join the river several miles away, and so I decided to follow that route. It was hot and I was dressed in my heavy uniform; soon, I was panting and perspiring, pausing every few yards to wipe my brow and regain my breath. I stopped every few minutes to rest, each time turning to view the panorama which was unfolding below me.

As I climbed higher and higher, I could see the entire dale spread below with all the farms, cottages, patchwork of fields and web of stone walls in view. I realized people from the cities and towns would have to pay heavily to see this kind of countryside. But I did not have time to daydream and revel in the landscape—I was hunting a truant! Unfortunately, I was not as fit as I should be—and certainly, not as agile as a ten-year-old boy would be. But I persisted, noting that it was now approaching one o'clock, and then as I crested yet another incline, I saw him. I saw the small figure of Simon Ellis sitting with his back to a dry stone wall which followed the line of the hill and he was gazing at something through his binoculars. He was sufficiently absorbed in his observations not to notice my arrival and I was able to approach him before he realized I was there. I thought he would get up and run, but he did not. His face, however, revealed his fear of my discovery.

'Hello, Simon,' I said, sitting at his side and resting my tired legs. 'What brings you up here?'

'Hello, Mr Rhea.' He licked his lips nervously, clearly wondering why I was here and what I was going to do. 'There's a silver hawk's nest down there,' and he pointed towards a hollow in the moor.

'Is it?' I was surprised. 'Are you sure?'

'Yes, it's got four eggs in, very light blue ones.'

'Has it? It's not a seagull of some kind, then?'

'No, Mr Rhea! I know what a seagull looks like!'

'Can you show me?'

'She's sitting on the eggs, Mr Rhea, we'd frighten her off. But the male will come soon to feed her, then you'll see where the nest is. It's near that big lump of rock, the one with the green moss on it, over there,' and he pointed.

I followed the line of his outstretched finger and found the boulder.

'So we wait?' I asked him.

'Yes, he'll be here soon, the silver hawk. You'll see him, Mr Rhea, but you must not tell anyone.'

'Mustn't I? Why not?'

'Because it's a very rare bird, Mr Rhea, and people mustn't know it's here ... it's come back, you see, back to Aidensfield. They used to live here a long time ago. This is Witch Hill, Mr Rhea, and they say the silver hawk brings good fortune to the people who live here ... ah, there

252

he is! Watch him, Mr Rhea, watch the silver hawk,' and he pointed to a dot in the sky, handing me his binoculars.

I focused them on the approaching bird and saw that it was a large bird of prey, heading towards me on slow-moving wings, almost gliding in fact. And it was silver. At least, it appeared to be silver where the bright sunshine touched its back, wings and underparts; I saw that it had black wing tips and that it was carrying something in its talons. Certainly, the sun appeared to be glinting from its plumage and I could see why it was called the silver hawk.

'He will call to his mate soon,' I heard Simon whisper to me. 'She'll rise from the nest to meet him ... you'll see.'

He was right.

As the beautiful shining silver hawk soared above the boulder Simon had indicated, it issued a sharp call and I saw a large brown bird rise from the ground, from a place hidden in the heather. As the silver hawk cried and called, she rose into the air to meet him and then did something remarkable. When she was flying directly beneath him, she turned over onto her back with her talons outstretched and at that stage, the male dropped his catch. It looked like a small bird, dead of course, but she deftly caught it in her claws, rolled over and flew back to the nest. The majestic silver bird executed a huge turn in the air and soared away towards the horizon, to find something else for his mate.

'That was amazing!' I handed the binoculars back to Simon. 'I had no idea birds did that!'

'The silver hawk does that,' he said. 'It is famous for it.'

'But the other bird was brown,' I pointed out.

'Yes, that is the female,' he told me with the authority of one who knew his subject. 'She sits on the eggs while he hunts, and if we approach the nest, she will attack us.'

'You know a lot about birds, Simon,' I said. 'I did not think there was such a bird as the silver hawk.'

'That's not its real name, Mr Rhea. I checked in books at school. It's a hen harrier, that's its real name. The male is white and grey with black tips to his wings, and the female is brown with dark streaks. They are very rare, Mr Rhea, we must not tell anyone about this.'

'Is that why you didn't go to school

today?' I put to him. 'Because you wanted to see the silver hawk?'

'I'm guarding it, Mr Rhea, guarding the nest in case people come to steal the eggs.'

'But no one's likely to do that, are they? They'll never find the nest, Simon, and if what you say is true, the female will drive them away!'

'They might shoot her, Mr Rhea, to steal the eggs.'

'Who might?' I asked, sensing there was something deeper in all this.

'Those two men in the tent,' he told me. 'I've seen them walking about the moor; I think they're looking for the nest.'

I didn't tell him that it would be a simple matter to find the nest if they really wanted—it was a matter of waiting for the male to return and for both birds to perform their spectacular aerobatics.

'Two men in a tent?' I asked. 'Where are they?'

'There are some trees over there, out of our sight, under the hill. They've got a tent near a small beck, and a motor bike.'

'Can you show me?' I asked.

'We mustn't scare the bird,' he said, rising to his feet to lead me over the

255

moors for half a mile or so. We moved into the shelter of one of the many dry stone walls which adorned Witch Hill and soon I was standing a short distance from a small green tent. A scrambles motor bike, adapted as a two-seater, was parked on its stand nearby.

'Are they there?' I asked Simon.

'No, they went off early,' he said, 'walking; I saw them through my binoculars.'

'Whereabouts?' I asked.

'Up to that farm over there.' He indicated an elevated farm at the far side of the dale. 'I saw them just before you came.'

I groaned. I knew the farm. It was called High Swang and belonged to Adam and Elizabeth Lonsdale. It was too far away to reach by foot and involved a seven or eight mile journey from here by car, so I decided to obtain the registration number of the bike and call the police station at Ashfordly via my police radio.

'What did they look like?' I asked him, without much hope.

'I saw them through my binoculars,' he said. 'One of them is very tall and thin and he has long, dirty hair. He wears jeans and a dark-blue shirt. The other was smaller and had glasses on, he had long hair as well, light brown.'

'Thanks, Simon, this is brilliant!'

With Simon watching, I made a quick search of the tent which revealed only a pair of sleeping bags and some personal belongings, with nothing to suggest a name for either of the men. But the bike did have a registration plate and I noted the number, the tax disc revealing it was registered in Middlesbrough.

'Simon, I must go to my car now, and ring for help. I want to catch those men whoever they are. Now, you have your bike, eh?'

'Yes, I must go now.'

'Simon, you must not stay away from school like this. Your mum and dad are frantic with worry, and Miss Preston too.'

'I had to protect the silver hawk, Mr Rhea, and daren't tell anybody.'

'Well, if I can find those two men, I think the silver hawk's nest will be safe. You can still come up here after school, and at weekends, and I do think we should tell the experts about the bird. I can tell everyone you were right in what you saw, that it's not a seagull of any kind.'

He walked at my side and when I reached his cycle, I realized I could remove the front wheel, and that it would then go in the rear of my Mini-van. I would carry him back to Aidensfield in my van. But before doing anything else, I raised Ashfordly Police on the radio. Alf Ventress answered.

'Alf,' I said, 'I'm on the moors near Witch Hill,' and then proceeded to explain about the thefts from the farms. I added my theories about the two suspects and said they were now thought to be in the vicinity of High Swang, on foot. I provided the registration details of the motor bike too, and he said he would check with Middlesbrough motor taxation department to ascertain the owner. I concluded by saying I would drop Simon Ellis off at his home in Aidensfield before taking the road out to High Swang, hopefully to catch two thieves. Alf said that there was a road traffic patrol car in the locality—it had called at Ashfordly Police Station only ten minutes earlier, and he would direct it to High Swang. If that happened, then I could return to wait near the little tent.

I then suggested Alf telephone the Lonsdales at High Swang to alert them to the presence of two possible villains—I knew that the farm had a bell extension from their phone, so they could hear it ringing if they were in the outbuildings, and if that sounded, it might scare off any potential thieves. Alf assured me he would do that. I eased to a halt outside Daniel Ellis's home and eased Simon's bike from the rear of my van before knocking on the door. Dan answered and the moment he saw his son, he started to shout at him.

'No, wait,' I pleaded with him. 'Your Simon has been doing some excellent work, Dan; apart from identifying a rare bird—a hen harrier—he's probably helped me catch a couple of thieves. So don't be hard on him—I've explained about not taking time off school without permission ... and I'll call later to explain in greater detail.'

'All right.' He did not sound too convinced, but calmed down as he led his son inside, leaving bike and its front wheel propped against the wall. Before deciding whether I should return to the tent and motor bike, or head for High Swang, I radioed Alf Ventress again.

'Tango Seven Seven is *en route* to High Swang,' he told me. 'Sergeant Blaketon suggests you return to their tent in case they make for it. I have contacted Middlesbrough Police with the name of the owner of the motor cycle; enquiries are being made from CID and a reply is awaited. Over.'

'Received and understood,' I responded, turning around and heading back to silver hawk country.

As I drove the long, slow miles to the foot of Witch Hill, I heard Tango Seven Seven report its arrival at High Swang where, it seemed, Adam Lonsdale had caught the two youths actually in the process of raiding his pantry. He'd held them at the point of his twelve bore until the arrival of the patrol car, and they were now being taken to Ashfordly Police Station under arrest for housebreaking. My presence was no longer required at the tent and so I turned around and made for Ashfordly, learning as I did so, that the owner of the bike was called Spike Blackburn and his companion was Steve Murphy, both petty crooks from Middlesbrough.

It seemed they were known to the local CID who said there had been some kind of trouble between rival gangs on Teesside, as a result of which these two likely lads had abandoned their usual haunts until the fuss died down. They had literally taken to the hills, but lacking the knowledge required to cater for themselves in the great British outback, they had raided farmhouses for food and some cash, the latter being used for trips into Ashfordly to buy fish and chips and the occasional pint of beer. They'd been in their tent for five days, but I think they were pleased to be arrested—at least they'd have a warm cell for tonight and some hot food, even if it did come from the fish and chip shop.

It was a successful conclusion to a curious but very interesting day—I learned something about ornithology and decided I would introduce Simon to a wildlife expert I knew in Pickering—the return of the silver hawk to our moors was too important to ignore, and it was Simon Ellis who had discovered the bird.

The hen harrier species, unfairly accused of raiding poultry runs, had almost become extinct in this country but once the bird received the protection of the law, its numbers began to increase. Once limited to the Orkneys and Outer Hebrides, it began to colonize parts of Great Britain after the war, all the time moving further south as its numbers increased. The sighting near Aidensfield was very important and, even now in the late 1990s, the hen harrier can be seen on the North York Moors.

For the farmers in the remote moors above Aidensfield, the return of the silver hawk had indeed provided some good fortune. In a roundabout sort of way, that spectacular and rare bird of prey had helped to catch those who were preying on its neighbours.

7 Horse Sense

Wrest once the law to your authority,
To do a great right, do a little wrong.
William Shakespeare (1564–1616)

Many of us conceal a sense of mischief or a desire to bc daring and this hidden deviousness can occasionally reveal itself in minor incidents of lawbreaking. There is something rather bold in breaking the law in a very minor way and not being found out, like sneaking a telephone call paid for by one's firm or taking home a pencil or paper clip from the office. In the minds of some people, there is excitement in committing minor misdeeds and getting away with it—such little villains would never stoop to serious crime like burglary, robbery or murder.

Stealing apples is probably the most common example, for illicitly obtained apples do taste far better than those bought in a shop. Exceeding the speed limit by a few miles per hour is perhaps another example, particularly if a police car passes in the opposite direction—we have broken the law and not been caught, another example of our personal bravado! It is important, of course, that no one is injured or harmed by such audacious behaviour.

Betting and gaming in the pub also involves the breaching of further laws, in this case those governing the conduct of licensed premises but probably the most frequent and popular instances of luscious law-breaking remains the drinking of alcoholic beverages in pubs when they are supposed to be closed.

This offence has always held a special appeal, probably because it happens so often in rural pubs. One of the ways in which an incomer to a village could recognize his acceptance by the community was when he was allowed to remain behind among the regulars to drink after time. In the sixties, there could be no doubt there was a brazen thrill in drinking in pubs after closing time—quite inexplicably, the drink tasted better, the conversation became more sparkling, the company grew more delightful by the minute and, of course, there was always the deep thrill of anticipation at the thought of a police raid.

The latter possibility is a further indication of our desire to appear fearless and fun-loving. Nonetheless, to prevent our den of iniquity being discovered, the pub doors were locked, the lights were turned low, tell-tale cars were removed from the car-park and conversation was kept to a low volume. All these strategic manoeuvres served to elevate the drinking to the level of a clandestine meeting, something shrouded in secrecy of which we became a willing part. There was no doubt a lot of people preferred this kind of gallantry to the thought of trekking to polar regions, discovering new continents or tackling the slopes of Everest. It was much easier to display one's true valour by buying a pint of bitter or a gin and tonic in an English pub after hours. If we were all genuine friends of the licensee, however, he could explain the late drinking by saying he was hosting a private party. That was quite legal, of course—he was perfectly entitled to host private parties in his own home but a pub full of regular customers paying for their own drinks after hours is hardly within the definition of a private party.

In permitting after-hours drinking, a licensee was risking his licence and thus his livelihood, these being additional elements of our display of great courage in the pursuit of illicit thrills. English law, in its infinite wisdom, has long recognized that the people of this country like to drink later than the general permitted hours. If the law *compelled* the public to drink at all hours, they would not want to do so but because restrictions are imposed, there is a general desire to find a way around the rules. This is revealed in the way the public liked to drink in pubs outside the normal licensing hours even during the daytime.

It must be said that drink taken in the romance of night tastes far better than that consumed during the daytime. Nonetheless, the law did provide an opportunity to drink all day, every day. This came from the delightful relaxations which applied to market towns on market days. For many years on those days, the pubs opened from around 10 a.m. and remained so until 11 p.m. with no closing period during the afternoon. This was officially known as a general order of exemption. Some called it a market-day licence. Dedicated drinkers would plan their weekly outings to coincide with market towns which had the benefit of a general order of exemption Harrowby Market was on a Monday, Galtreford was on a Tuesday, Brantsford on a Wednesday, Eltering on a Thursday, Ashfordly on a Friday with Thirsk, Malton and Northallerton using Saturday for their markets. Thus a dedicated boozer, with the aid of Arnold Merryweather's country bus service, could drink fairly locally all day on every day of the week, except Sunday which was a day of rest.

In spite of availability of these opportunities, the drinking public always tried to find other ways of drinking outside permitted hours, and in some cases ingenuity was deployed. I liked the story of the dales village of Rammington. Once a busy market town, it had slowly reverted to being a small village and the weekly Thursday market had ceased almost two centuries ago. The market-place was now a car-park. An enterprising landlord who owned the Black Ram Inn discovered that a charter for the weekly market had been given to the town by Edward III in 1352 and he reckoned it had established for all time that Rammington was a market town. This being so, he reasoned, it should have a market, and in furtherance of that, the pubs should be allowed to remain open all day. To give him his due, he did persuade one or two traders to position stalls on the former market-place—the WI sold cakes and jam, a woodturner sold bowls and bread boards and a model maker put model aircraft on sale. This, argued the landlord, constituted a market, and so he applied to the magistrates for a general order of exemption which would permit the pubs in Rammington to remain open from 10 a.m. until 11 p.m., to cater for the refreshment of the market traders. When his application was heard by the local magistrates, they expressed a learned opinion that three trestle tables, recently introduced to the car-park, did not really constitute a market whereupon the landlord said that the real market was in his pub. That's where the traders could congregate to engage in their trading—if the exemption was approved, his pub would be full of farmers and dealers, but the magistrates decided, albeit with some reluctance, that deals done in the bar of a pub did not constitute a market of that kind envisaged by Edward III.

They also reasoned that the three stalls on the car-park did not conform to

Edward's concept of a market either. So the application was rejected. Nonetheless, it did illustrate the burning desire within English folk to drink outside licensing hours and it also revealed something of the lengths to which they will go to achieve that purpose. Perhaps the most simple way to legally achieve after-hours drinking, other than tippling at home, was for a pub to apply for a special order of exemption.

In my time at Aidensfield, the law relating to drinking alcohol was being relaxed—pubs could stay open until 11 p.m. instead of 10.30 p.m., the ten-minute drinking-up time was introduced, a half-hour drinking-up time with a meal was permitted, pubs with restaurants could serve drinks with meals until midnight and licensed restaurants were permitted. In spite of all that, people still wanted to drink in their favourite pubs outside the permitted hours and the special order of exemption allowed this.

It was, and still is, more commonly known as an extension of hours. It can be granted to the licensee of a pub, but only when there is a special occasion to celebrate. Examples would include a wedding party on the premises, the annual dinner of a local organization or some other event which was considered 'special'. If the order was approved by the magistrates, it meant the pub could remain open after hours, perhaps until midnight, 1 a.m. or even 2 a.m.

If there were problems, they arose through interpretation of the word 'special' and the law seems content to let local magistrates decide what is 'special'.

Is New Year's Eve 'special' when it comes around once a year with surprising speed and regularity? And how about Christmas or Boxing Day? Are they 'special' enough to persuade the magistrates to let pubs remain open outside normal permitted hours? Test cases have included pubs wanting to remain open late for the annual Christmas late-night shopping, to watch the General Election results on television, or for customers to watch televised programmes in the early hours, such as the Olympics or a boxing championship from America.

Over the years, the word 'special' has been interpreted as meaning something special to the locality, although it can embrace something special of national status like a royal birth or a royal wedding. Such celebratory moments are both local and national, and this particular provision has been developed to include local weddings and wedding anniversary celebrations such as golden or silver parties, twenty-first or eighteenth birthdays, village shows, annual dinners for local organizations and other worthy causes. In all cases, they provide a basis for legally drinking alcohol in pubs after the normal permitted hours. The problem is that this overwhelming desire to drink later than permitted by law has led to requests for odd events to be declared special enough to justify a late-drinking extension of hours.

The ancient sport of dwyle-flonking was introduced in the 1960s, the annual championship being regarded as special enough to warrant an extension of hours. This sport ranks alongside others like rhubarb-thrashing, marrow-dangling, passing the splod, dratting and nurgling, ferret-legging, nettle-wrestling, flither-picking or even conger-cuddling.

All these, and more, might be regarded as special enough in their localities to justify drinking outside normal permitted hours. When these activities are quoted as being special reasons for wanting to drink after hours, it is really just another ingenious excuse to satisfy the overpowering need among the English to drink late in a pub.

So far as the various pubs on my patch were concerned, all applied on regular occasions for extensions of hours. The reasons were commonplace and so there was no objection by the police—the events included the annual presentation of trophies by Aidensfield Cricket Club, Elsinby WI's annual dinner, various birthday and wedding celebrations, the famous Crampton tug-of-war contest, Briggsby's annual garden fête, Thackerston point-to-point meeting and many similar events and worthy celebrations. Elsinby's pub, the Hopbind, was noted as a venue for horse-racing enthusiasts; several horse-racing journalists lived in or near the village, consequently special events at the pub included many linked with racing. An annual dinner for judges at the various North Riding racecourses was an example, for which an extension of hours was always approved. Another nearby pub, just off my patch, was patronized by glider pilots who had their own special events—there were many similar examples of what can legitimately be regarded as 'special'.

In my own experience at Aidensfield, no one ever attempted to dream up a daft reason for making application for an extension of hours and so, when George Ward, landlord of the Hopbind Inn hailed me in the street one morning I had no reason to even consider any deviousness.

He told me he would be applying to the magistrates for a special order of exemption. I could never envisage dwyle-flonking in my local pubs, although I do believe the occasional bout of dratting and nurgling was practised. One local inn on the moors has a wonderful collection of nurgling sticks and dratting poles while another was the venue of the annual egg-waltzing contest.

'Morning, Nick.' George was on his way to the post office when he spotted me. 'I'll be applying for an extension at next week's court. It's for Friday the twelfth of next month. I'll be asking for my hours to be extended from eleven p.m. until one a.m. It's a birthday party; we'll provide a buffet supper with it.'

'I can't see anyone could object to that,' I said.

'I'll make application in the usual way,

through Sergeant Blaketon. I thought you ought to know.'

'Right, thanks. So whose birthday is it?' I asked. 'A special one by the sound of things?'

'A twenty-ninth,' he smiled.

'A twenty-ninth?' I frowned. 'That's a funny one to mark with a special celebration. I can understand somebody having a party for their twenty-first or thirtieth, but a twenty-ninth?'

'It is a bit special, Nick, so I was told,' George said. 'It's for somebody called Doctor Thorne; he's not expected to live much longer, a dicky heart I think. I got a phone call about it; apparently there's some local connection with Aidensfield.'

'Thorne?' I puzzled over the name.

I did not know anyone of that name in this area. Certainly, there was no doctor of that name living nearby but twenty-nine was a very young age, even for a qualified doctor. He was probably a house doctor in one of the local hospitals. Reading between the lines, I gained the impression that even someone as young as that, with a fatal illness, would want to return to his roots before leaving this world. It sounded like a sad reason for a celebration but I saw no reason to object. In my view, it did fit the criteria of 'special' and I told George I would mention it to Sergeant Blaketon; it was he who would present the application to the magistrates at their next sitting in Eltering. Later that day, I met Sergeant Blaketon at one of my rendezvous points and told him about George's forthcoming application.

Like me, Sergeant Blaketon was somewhat puzzled by a twenty-ninth birthday but he appreciated the reason when I explained it. I said it was a man called Doctor Thorne.

'Do you know this man, Rhea?' he asked.

'No, Sergeant,' I admitted.

'Well, I do remember him, Rhea. It's a sad story, though, but I shall not raise any objections to the application,' and there was a smile on his face as he said that. In due course, the necessary application came from George and I was present in Eltering Court, being a witness to a careless driving charge, when the application was heard. The clerk of the magistrates, Mr Eldred Whimp, dealt with several similar applications before the hearing of criminal cases and when it came to George's, he asked of Sergeant

Blaketon, 'Sergeant, there is an application for a special order of exemption from the Hopbind Inn, Elsinby on the occasion of a birthday party. The licensee wishes to have his hours extended from eleven until one o'clock the following morning. Is this a special birthday party?'

'It is indeed, Your Worships,' beamed Sergeant Blaketon. 'It is to celebrate the twenty-ninth birthday of a Doctor Thorne who is not expected to live much longer. A heart condition, I understand. I consider that to be a special occasion, one which is well within the terms of section 74(4) of the Licensing Act of 1964. The police have no objection to the application.'

'All right, Sergeant,' said Alderman Fazakerly, the chairman of the bench. 'Thank you. Any objections from the bench?' and he turned to the other members of his court. Mrs Pinkerton and Mr Smithers each signified their agreement and thus the application was approved.

'Application approved,' said Alderman Fazakerly. 'Now, Sergeant, a careless driving charge, I believe?'

'Yes, Your Worships, this defendant has pleaded guilty,' and so the business of Eltering Magistrates court got under way with the various guilty pleas being considered first. But George had had his application approved.

I thought no more about the event until the day of Doctor Thorne's birthday party. Sergeant Blaketon rang to remind me that the Hopbind Inn had an extension of hours that evening and, as was our practice on such occasions, he suggested I patrol the village as the extended hours came to a conclusion.

The purpose was to remind the licensee and the revellers that this extra drinking time was considered something of a privilege and that it should not be abused by unruly behaviour. There was also the question of ensuring no one drove their cars while under the influence of alcohol or made a nuisance of themselves in the street. Supplementing the flow and water level of Elsinby Beck was not permitted either, however urgent the need. I knew that George would never give me cause for alarm and that most of his customers were not prone to creating problems for me; I could not account for the guests at Doctor Thorne's birthday party however, and in any case, orders were orders. I assured Sergeant Blaketon I would attend, even though it meant another late night on duty.

'I might just drive out to give you a visit too,' was his concluding remark with a twinkle in his eye. 'It would be nice to renew my acquaintance with Doctor Thorne. That's if he is well enough to attend.'

As Elsinby church clock was striking midnight, I parked my Mini-van in Church Lane, nicely out of sight of the inn, and decided to take a walk around the village before visiting the Hopbind Inn. It was always prudent to show one's uniform in the bar on such occasions and I thought it would be nice to give birthday greetings to Doctor Thorne. When I walked past the pub, it was brightly lit and producing sounds of happiness from within. There was no music, I noted, but the noise of chatter and laughter made me realize the place was packed and everyone was enjoying themselves. Outside, the car-park and streets were full of expensive cars.

I noted Rovers, Jaguars, a Daimler, several sports cars and a wide range of up-market saloons. Many had racehorse mascots on their bonnets and racecourse passes in their windscreens, an indication that Doctor Thorne's friends were keen followers of the sport of kings. It was a fair bet he was a man of the turf too.

Outside the pub, there was no sign of trouble. No drunks lurked in doorways or watered the grass verges, the cars were all parked correctly with lights where required and I decided I was really superfluous here. But Sergeant Blaketon was *en route* which meant I had to wait for him. Rather than enter the pub twice, I decided to await his arrival, and we'd enter together, a token visit and display of the forces of law and order. Meanwhile, I occupied myself with a walk around Elsinby, checking the post office, shop, school and churches for security and soon I saw the familiar shape of Sergeant Blaketon's little black Ford. He halted outside the Hopbind Inn as I flashed my torch from a distance to show I was aware of his presence. He climbed out and walked towards me.

'All quiet, Rhea?' he asked the routine question.

'All quiet in the street, Sergeant, a bit noisy in there!' I laughed.

'No trouble, I hope!' he commented.

'Not a bit,' I assured him. 'It's all very good natured, and there are some very smart cars there. Racing folk, I believe. They're giving Doctor Thorne a good party.'

'Then we shall not intrude, Rhea. I think a quick look into the pub, to be recorded in the register of visits to licensed premises, will be sufficient. You and I will go in, make our presence known to George and leave.'

'I thought you wanted to meet Doctor Thorne?' I reminded him.

'If he's there, which I doubt. But yes, it would be nice to see him again. I will introduce you, Rhea,' and again I noticed a twinkle in his eye. Together, we strode towards the front door, moved along the passage and then into the large bar. It was packed solid with people all talking and laughing; many were strangers to me but among them were several local people, all horse-racing enthusiasts, and among them I noticed Claude Jeremiah Greengrass. Then one of the revellers spotted our uniforms.

'Here come the police horses!' chuckled someone.

'Size fifteen shoes,' laughed another.

'Fancy a drink, gentlemen?' asked one of the more sober among them.

'No thanks, not on duty,' Blaketon answered firmly, and then George made his way towards us from behind the bar. 'Evening, George.'

'Hello Sergeant; PC Rhea,' smiled George. 'A nice party. No trouble. I'll get them out on time, Sergeant. They're all in a good humour, there'll be no bother.'

'Good,' smiled Blaketon. 'Well, is Doctor Thorne here tonight?'

'We're bringing him in right now, he looks fit enough to attend,' said a man with a horsy face. 'You'll stay to hear us sing "Happy Birthday" to him, and join a toast?'

'Well, I hardly think we should,' I heard myself say with my sergeant's presence very much in mind. 'Not under the circumstances ...'

'Nonsense!' the man bellowed. 'This is a celebration, gentlemen, a celebration spanning more than quarter of a century of success and hard work. I know you're on duty but, in the circumstances, I think a glass of wine or sherry would not be out of order, not on such an important and sentimental occasion.'

I knew that Sergeant Blaketon followed his own very strict code of practice when on duty and yet he also had a warm heart. I knew he felt deeply for the doctor whose last party this might be but I was still surprised when he said, 'All right, on this one occasion. A dry sherry please and something for the constable.'

'Same for me,' I followed, still puzzling about his uncharacteristic behaviour.

'Get him in!' called our host as George organized the sherry, and there was a cheer followed by a lull in the proceedings. Quite unexpectedly, everyone in the bar became silent as someone went to find Doctor Thorne.

'Where is he?' I asked George.

'In the yard outside, he's been very good.'

George's comments puzzled me and I saw Blaketon raise his eyebrows and smile at me with just a hint of mystery as he accepted the glass of sherry; I took mine and waited. There was an air of expectancy now, and then someone gave the signal and the entire gathering started to sing. The bar was filled with a rendition of "Happy Birthday to You" as the rear door opened. And in came a racehorse.

Now I realized whose birthday it was. It was the horse's. And Sergeant Blaketon was staring at the animal, transfixed.

The sleek and still handsome gelding was led into the bar as everyone rose to their feet and continued the birthday song. The noise and presence of people did not worry the animal—racehorses do tend to become accustomed to the closeness of humans and the celebratory noises they create. I watched in silence, wondering how Sergeant Blaketon would react to celebrating a horse's birthday then realized he was singing with the rest of them. When the song was over, a man at the back said, 'Happy Birthday, Doctor Thorne' and raised his glass. We all did likewise, toasting Doctor Thorne who stood among us all calmly and without any show of fear or anxiety.

'Thanks George,' said Blaketon putting down his empty glass. 'A very nice party. Come on, Rhea, I've seen what I want to. It's time for us to leave.'

I followed him outside, fully expecting to be given a roasting, but he said, 'Rhea, what a brilliant idea, to celebrate that horse's birthday. I know it's not the first of January, when horses have their official birthdays, but by Jove, that horse was a good 'un. Do you know I once won fifty pounds on Doctor Thorne ... the Ebor it was, rank outsider he was then, but he proved himself. Wonderful animal, Rhea. Twenty-nine, eh, and still looking good even if his heart is a bit dicky. A big age for a horse, Rhea ...'

'Sarge,' I said as I walked at his side, 'did you know the party was for a horse?'

'Yes, of course I did. Didn't you?'

'Well,' I tried to flannel my way out of this, 'I knew it was something special, otherwise you wouldn't have allowed the application to go ahead ...'

'I recognized the name, Rhea, and I know the racing tradition which surrounds the Hopbind. But those magistrates had no idea,' he chuckled. 'But it was a special occasion, Rhea, and it was quite lawful. If the application had not been within the law, I should have objected, but in my opinion it was a special occasion within the meaning of the Licensing Act.'

He was always full of surprises, and it was clear that he had enjoyed my slight discomfiture. But as we walked to his car, I heard panting and footsteps behind. I turned to find Claude Jeremiah Greengrass and Alfred trying to catch us.

'Sergeant Blaketon,' cried Claude, 'can I have a word?'

'You can, Mr Greengrass,' beamed Blaketon, surprisingly affable towards his old adversary. 'What can we do for you?'

'That party.' Claude indicated the pub with a nod of his head. 'I mean, well, it was for a horse, George got permission to hold it for a horse, so well, I mean to say, it's Alfred's birthday next month and I wondered if, well, you know, I could hold a party for him and have George get an extension of licensing hours ...'

'You want to hold a party for that scruffy dog and get Their Worships to grant an extension of hours, a special order of exemption that is, for the sale and consumption of intoxicants on licensed premises outside permitted hours? All for a dog?'

'Aye, summat like that.'

'Right, let's start at the beginning. Have you got a licence for him?' asked Blaketon. 'A dog licence, I mean.'

Claude halted in his tracks. 'Aye, well, mebbe it wasn't such a good idea,' he blinked. 'You can't expect a countryman's dog to spend his life

285

dominated by licences, can you, Sergeant? It's licences for this and licences for that ...'

'And licences if you want to booze late with your hound. Give him a treat at home; he might like a night in once in a while. Good night, Claude,' grinned Blaketon. 'And good night, PC Rhea.'

And as Claude shuffled into the darkness, I heard Blaketon's parting words to me, 'If he gets an extension of hours for his dog's birthday, we'll have rabbits, budgies and gerbils applying to have parties here. We have to uphold the dignity of the law, Rhea. Remember that. Thoroughbred horses are one thing, mongrels and lurchers are another.'

'Yes, Sergeant,' I said, 'But before you go, who was Doctor Thorne? That horse must have been named after someone!'

'Anthony Trollope, Rhea! Have you read Trollope? It's the title of the third of his Barsetshire novels—you should read more, Rhea, then you would know more.'

'Yes, Sergeant. I will, thank you and good night.'

'Good night, Rhea,' and I watched as he entered his car and drove away.

If the village of Elsinby had a strong horse-racing tradition, then the entire county of the North Riding of Yorkshire catered well for those who followed the sport.

There were several racecourses within its boundaries, all policed by the North Riding Constabulary. They included Thirsk, Catterick, Thornaby, Redcar and, by an accident of geography, York's famous track on the Knavesmire. In the neighbouring Ridings there were other convenient courses, such as Beverley, Ripon, Wetherby, Doncaster and Pontefract, with others in Durham and Northumberland, such as Sedgefield and Hexham. Added to this galaxy of horse-racing venues there were several point-to-point meetings, and for those with an interest in the history of horse-racing, the North Riding could offer historic but disused courses at Richmond, Middleham, Northallerton and Hambleton among others. There is also the famous Kiplingcoates Derby in East Yorkshire. This is England's oldest horse race which continues to be staged in March every year over its four and a half miles course. The course is officially flat—but try telling that to the riders and their mounts!

If horse-racing was not of interest, there

was an opportunity to watch motor-racing at several disused airfields, speed boat racing off the coast, massed start cycle-racing and time trials on the roads, motor rallies in the forests and on the moors, motor-cycle scrambles on farm land and rough terrain, athletics and swimming at several places including many of our schools, aerobatics and jet aircraft in action at several airfields plus the calm of gliding from Sutton Bank Top. The Yorkshire rail network boasts two of the longest stretches of straight railway line in this country—one runs for more than twenty miles absolutely straight from near Thirsk to York and the other some eighteen miles from Barlby in North Yorkshire to Brough in East Yorkshire, each ideal for testing the speeds of railway engines.

There is a good deal of high speed rail history in the county. That wonderful record-breaking steam engine, the world famous Mallard (No. 60022) which broke the world record for steam (126 m.p.h.) in 1938 can occasionally still be seen chugging along some Yorkshire routes, including the North York Moors steam railway near Goathland. Officially, though, she now lives in graceful retirement in

York's National Railway Museum, having undergone a thorough restoration.

There are some long, straight stretches of road too, and some of these are used by the police as their officially approved 'measured mile'. The measured mile was used by police drivers to check the accuracy of their speedometers—whenever a police officer appeared in court as a witness against a speeding driver, the speedo of the police vehicle involved was checked by timing with a stop watch its movement along a measured mile. The drive was witnessed and certified, and this was done to counter any allegations of mechanical inaccuracy which might come from the defendant in court.

The roads of our country, however, are not constructed for motor- or cycle-racing. Indeed, as a general rule, such speed trials on public roads are forbidden, although there are some exceptions. Mass start cycle-racing or time trials for cycles are permitted under certain circumstances and with some conditions. Motor rallies generally occur off the roads and are usually neutralized as they pass along the public highway. In some cases, there are provisions for roads to be temporarily closed to the public to permit the passage of a cycle race or other event.

These wide-ranging and varied facilities, one would expect, are sufficient to cater for all those who want to enjoy the adrenalin of racing in all its legal forms, in whatever style it is done. Quite literally, the North Riding had something for everyone. One essential part of horse-racing, however, was the opportunity to place a wager on the outcome, something not applicable to all the pastimes I have highlighted. And placing a bet was something akin to the compulsion for drinking after hours that I have mentioned earlier in this chapter. If punters could not do it legally, they would find all manner of excuses to do so illegally. In spite of that, I often felt that our county provided every kind of racing pastime.

That is, except for a scheme devised by Claude Jeremiah Greengrass.

My first intimation that something odd was going on came with a complaint from the driver of a milk tanker. He knocked on my door at 8.30 one summer morning and I invited him into the office. His name was Arthur Fletcher and he worked for Ashfordly Dairies; I knew him by sight for he was one of the regular users of the roads on my patch.

'So, what's the trouble, Arthur?' I asked.

'This morning,' he said, 'just after half-past five as I was starting my pick-up run, these three idiots on horses nearly caused an accident. I had to swerve like hell to avoid 'em ... all over t'road they were. I thought you ought to know. I thought I wouldn't knock you out of bed at that time of day, anyway I was just starting off and it's a tight schedule, so I blasted my horn at 'em and kept going. I'm telling you now, on my home run.'

'Racehorses undergoing training, were they?' I asked, for there was a number of training establishments around my beat. They never galloped on the roads, however, although they could often be seen walking towards the turf they used for training.

'Gypsies more like,' he told me. 'Skew-bald ponies, shaggy things. Not racehorses, Nick, not in a million years.'

'There are some gypsies camping on the verge near Stovensby, not far from the disused airfield,' I said. 'They seem to come every year about this time. I noticed several ponies and caravans, they have skewbalds among them.'

'It'll be them, they'll be heading for Appleby Horse Fair,' he said.

'Is that where you saw the horses? Near Stovensby Airfield?'

'Not far away,' he nodded. 'Between there and Brantsford, there's a long straight stretch of road with a telephone kiosk on the corner. They came belting down there, side by side, going like hell. Like the Charge of the Light Brigade it was, or summat from a spaghetti western. They met me as I came out of the side road.'

'That's the measured mile,' I said, and explained the significance of that piece of road.

'Well, I have no names or description other than skewbald horses, but I thought a word of warning might not be amiss.'

'I'll have words with them later this morning,' I assured him, and off he went. Upon his departure, I racked my brains to determine whether or not horse-racing was illegal on public roads.

The only reference I found was one which said it was an offence to ride on any street so as to endanger life or limb and another which stated that it was illegal to ride any horse furiously so as to endanger the life or limb of anyone using the road.

One interesting fact with the latter offence was that the fine was doubled if the rider of the horse was also the owner.

During my morning patrol, I motored towards Stovensby. I took the route through Crampton which meant passing the disused airfield which spread across the base of the dale as a mess of broken and abandoned concrete runways. Once a busy airfield, it served the country well during World War II, but was now a mess of derelict buildings, a tatty control tower and abandoned runways which sprouted thistles and other weeds. An ideal place for a gypsies to use, I thought as I made for the gypsy encampment.

As I approached, I became aware of about a dozen horse-drawn caravans with rounded tops, wagon-type bases and tin chimneys sticking up like periscopes; some two dozen skewbald, piebald or dappled ponies and horses were tethered to metal pins which had been hammered into the ground. The animals were grazing along the wide grass verge and were spread out across a considerable distance. I knew I would be unwelcome here. Gypsies, whether the true Romany people or that multitude of mobile tinkers who pretend to be members of that race, tend to be very wary of police officers. They would think I was coming to move them along or serve summonses for something or other.

I had no thoughts of antagonism towards them, and had had no complaints about their presence or behaviour, other than the horse-racing allegation. I knew that true gypsies were a wonderful, clean and honourable race of people but that their open-air lifestyle had been emulated by less savoury characters. There were times it was not easy to decide which was which.

Parking my Mini-van at a discreet distance, I walked slowly towards the encampment, noting the smoke rising from one or two fires, kettles and pans hanging from hooks, the women and children sitting around in the morning sunshine and a few menfolk standing around and talking or sitting on the steps of their wagons. Some other women appeared to be working in the caravans. I sought the leader of this group but knew that if I asked for their names, they would all be called something like Malachi Smith of no fixed abode. During my long walk, I was kept under observation by the men, some of whom were smoking clay pipes.

'Good morning,' I said, smiling in what I hoped was a welcoming way. There was no reply. I stood my ground.

'I am PC Rhea, the village constable from Aidensfield.' I tried to make some contact. 'I have received a complaint about horses racing on the road this morning, the road over there,' and I pointed in the general direction of the measured mile. Again there was no response, merely steadfast and unsmiling faces looking at me. 'I am not here to move you on,' I tried. 'I just wanted to say that there was almost an accident this morning, if they were your animals, they could have been injured or killed. If you race the animals on the road, they could be injured.'

This sparked off some kind of animated discussion between several of the men but I could not understand a word because they spoke in a foreign language. I guessed it was Romany, the tongue gypsies adopt when confronted by authority or when they anticipated danger. Then one of them, a man in his late forties with dark skin and very thick, black hair, said in English, 'We were told it was in order, mister. The roads are quiet at that time of day. No cars. No people.'

'Who told you that?'

'The man Greengrass.' And I groaned aloud at the mention of his name. 'He is doing a deal with us, he said it would be all right.'

'Very little said by Mr Greengrass is all right!' I smiled ruefully.

'But there is no law against horses using the roads, is there?' The man was smiling at me now. I felt I had made some kind of progress.

'No, there is no law to stop horses using the road, but there are laws to stop them being ridden furiously and to the danger of others on the road,' I said. 'You can trot them or gallop them, but not race them.'

'I see no difference, mister,' he frowned. 'Walking, galloping, racing ...'

'Racing can lead to danger, to the horses as well as other road users, and so our law says it is illegal.'

'Even at five thirty on a light summer morning when no one is around?' he said.

'If there was no one around, we should not know about it,' I laughed. 'It is because someone was around, in a lorry, that has made me aware of it. I am here to ask you to stop, for the sake of your animals and other road users.'

He smiled slyly at me and said, 'But they were not all our horses, mister.'

I knew that it would be extremely difficult to prove whether any of the galloping horses belonged to this group, and he knew that.

'So whose were they?' I returned.

'One is ours, the other two belong to Mr Greengrass,' he said.

'Greengrass?' I looked at the animals spread along the verge.

'You mean most of these belong to Claude?'

'No, not these. These are all ours. Two of the three galloping this morning belong to Mr Greengrass.'

'I don't understand.' I was puzzled by this statement and for a moment did not believe what I was hearing.

'We need to complete a deal with Mr Greengrass,' he said. 'We are people of our word. The gallops must continue, for four more days.'

'So what is this deal? Why is it so important?' I put to him.

'You know Greengrass, mister?'

'I do indeed,' I said with emphasis.

'He buys and sells horses, among other things.'

'Does he?' I had no idea he dealt in horses. Not thoroughbreds, I felt.

'He keeps them somewhere, horses like ours, horses that sell in horse fairs. We sell his horses for him, at Appleby Horse Fair. It follows at the end of this month.'

'You sell all his horses?' I was surprised at this.

'No, we agree to take five of them to Appleby for him. Five of his best ones. That is all we can cope with. So, he selects ten of his best horses and brings them to us. We gallop them as happened this morning, to see which is the best. One of ours goes with them; ours are fit animals, mister. Being on the road all days keeps them fit. We compare his with ours. And we take his five best ones to Appleby, get the best price and return the proceeds, less our commission and expenses, to Greengrass when we come here next time, after Appleby.'

'But surely,' I said, 'there are other ways of assessing the condition of a horse?'

'Of course, mister. We check them all, but we need to know they are fit for the walk to Appleby, and after that, they will be fit for sale. I can tell a lot from a one mile gallop, none of his has ever beaten ours in the morning race.'

'One mile?'

'Greengrass said the place we use is exactly one mile long, used by the police to test their cars, he told us.'

'He's right. We test our speedometers on that measured mile, but I never dreamt it could be used to establish the condition of a horse. So I'd better have words with Mr Greengrass. Was he there this morning?'

'Yes, he was with us. Our men were the riders of all the horses, mister. We know our horses. And we shall pick the five best of his to take with us.'

'Well, I cannot give you permission to race your horses on the road.'

'If we could find another place with a mile of level going, we would prefer to use it,' he said.

'You've tried the old airfield, it's just along the road from here?'

'No,' he said. 'We do not ask any more. We are always turned away.'

'If I could secure you permission to race your horses on that old airstrip, would that suit you?'

He smiled and nodded. 'That would be very much appreciated. It is only once a year.'

'I'll go right away,' I promised him.

The owner of the derelict airfield was a farmer called Humphrey Grisedale whom I knew well. A sober gentleman, devoted Methodist and teetotaller, he led a very pure kind of life, never visiting the local pub, never going to whist drives or supporting charities which involved hunting, shooting or fishing. Tall and slim with a skull-like face, he answered my knock with a wide and toothy smile for which he was renowned.

'Mr Rhea,' he beamed. 'How good of you to call. What can I do for you this time?'

'It's not a stock register visit,' I said. 'More of a request for assistance.'

'Well, you know me, a Christian gentleman through and through. I always help those in need,' he said with one of his wide smiles.

I commented upon his known philanthropic work in the district and followed it with a commentary upon the dangers present upon our highways. Having, hopefully, paved the way for a sympathetic reception to my request, I went on, 'Mr Grisedale,' I said. 'Some acquaintances of mine need a length of smooth, flat terrain upon which to test the quality of their livestock. Horses, in fact. They need a goodly distance—a mile is about right—and it would be required for about five days during the year, five consecutive days. Currently, they are using the public highway for this ... I feel it is very dangerous and probably unlawful, but I wonder if you would consider allowing them to use the old runways which you now own.'

'Has Greengrass been talking to you, Mr Rhea?' he frowned as he put the question to me.

'Greengrass? No, he hasn't. Why?'

'Well, he came to me some time ago, a year or two since in fact, with exactly the same proposition. Something to do with grading horses for sale at Appleby Fair, if I remember rightly.'

'Yes, that sounds like it. And what was your reaction?'

'Outright refusal, Mr Rhea. No chance.'

'Oh,' was all I could think of saying, before adding, 'Can I ask why?'

'Gambling, Mr Rhea. I am steadfastly opposed to any form of gambling. It is sinful, in my view, and Greengrass was placing bets on the horses which he told me about ... so I refused. Betting is against my religion and my principles.'

'So if I persuaded Greengrass to avoid any form of gambling when dealing with the horses, you might reconsider it?'

'I am a Christian gentleman, Mr Rhea, and if I have the facilities on my land to avoid the risk of injury or accident, then of course I shall be pleased to assist.'

'Gypsies are involved.' I had to be fair with this man. 'They are camping along the lane now.'

'I have no objection to genuine Romanies, Mr Rhea. Those people down the lane are genuine, I have seen them and talked to them. Indeed, if only they would ask, I should be happy for them to camp in the southeastern corner of my old airfield. It is land without any other function, they could have it and be settled. You will tell them that?'

'I'll explain about the no-gambling and no-betting condition ... so you have a long stretch of runway they can use?'

'I have, Mr Rhea. I have indeed.'

When I returned to the gypsy encampment and spoke to the man with whom I had the earlier conversation, he was delighted.

'The Greengrass man told me to avoid the airfield,' he said. 'He said the man was not human ...'

'The man is human in his own way,' I smiled. 'But his religious beliefs forbid gambling of any kind. You go and see him ... I will go and see Greengrass.'

'Thank you mister,' he said, holding out his hand for me to shake.

'I'm PC Rhea, Aidensfield Police,' I reminded him.

'Malachi Smith, at your service,' he smiled in return.

I shrugged my shoulders at that response, returned to my Mini-van and went off to find Claude Jeremiah Greengrass. He was working on his ranch when I arrived, collecting eggs from one of his battered henhouses.

'Now then, Claude,' I called as I emerged from my van.

'I didn't do it, whatever it is,' he called. 'And Alfred didn't worry that lad's pet hamster.'

'What hamster?' I asked.

'Whose ever hamster it was that got worried,' he grinned. 'Anyroad, what brings you here this fine summer morning?'

'Horse-racing on the highway, Claude.

Contrary to section 78 of the Highways Act 1835. You nearly caused a milk tanker to have a pile-up this morning.'

'I wasn't riding the damned things, it was them gyppos.'

'But they were your horses, Claude. Well, two of them were, two out of three. It's got to stop!'

'It's business, Constable.' He blinked at me and twisted his head around in his nervousness. 'I have to sell 'em, and I have to show they're good horses, for Appleby. Those gyppos want to see 'em race, hold their own against their animals ...'

'Then do it on the old airfield,' I said.

'He won't let us, old skinflint Grisedale.'

'He will, if you don't gamble on the outcome.' I tried very hard not to smile at this stage.

'Gamble? Who said owt about gambling?'

'It is an offence to loiter on a street or public place for the purpose of placing bets,' I chanted at him. 'So if I turn up on the measured mile in the morning and find you racing horses on the highway and placing bets on the outcome, you'd finish up in Ashfordly police cells. Want to bet on that?'

He readjusted his neck and blinked his eyes and said, 'Who do I see about all this?'

'Grisedale for one, and Malachi Smith for another.'

'Who?'

'The gypsy leader. Malachi Smith.'

'His name's Seamus O'Flaherty,' grinned Claude. 'Malachi Smith ...'

'All gypsies are called Malachi Smith,' I chuckled. 'Even those who speak to policemen!'

'Aye, well, I suppose I ought to thank you, getting us off the road. I mean, if Sergeant Blaketon had come round that corner instead of a milk tanker, well, you never know, do you?'

'I do know, Claude, which is why I recommend you accept Grisedale's offer. Horse-racing on his old runways yes! Betting on the outcome, no!'

'Can I sell you a good horse?' he chuckled. 'One owner, low mileage, economical ...'

'Only if it's comprehensively insured,' I retorted, and left him.

But in the days which followed, horses ridden by gypsies raced around the old airfield at Stovensby before being selected for sale at one of the country's most famous horse fairs. And now, the tradition continues. It's much more formalized now with lots more horses and riders taking part. The Stovensby Horse Trials are an annual event, but bookmakers are still not allowed on the track. That is also a tradition, even though poor old Humphrey Grisedale died several years ago. The old airfield is under new management now.

Claude Jeremiah Greengrass gets a complimentary ticket, however. And so do I.

8   To the Woods

We must never assume that which is
incapable of proof.
> *George Henry Lewes* (1817–1878)

One of the chief lessons learned at
a police training school is that one
should never make assumptions without
the necessary supporting evidence. For a
police officer, therefore, the gathering of
material evidence is vital if an allegation of
wrongdoing is to be supported, especially
in court. One should never prosecute a
person without the necessary evidence,
although arrests can be made upon a
basis of reasonable suspicion.

There are times however, when the
desired evidence is not easy to obtain
or even beyond the range of the most
diligent investigatory efforts, consequently
even the best police officer in the world
may reach a conclusion which, in the light
of future events, is proved inaccurate or
even downright wrong. Members of the

general public are not bound by such a rigid discipline, though, and there are times when a set of circumstances which is observed by them can lead to assumptions which are totally untrue. Gossips are wonderful examples of this—they can witness a small incident and dream up all manner of dubious 'facts' from their interpretation of what they saw. It is frankly amazing how often people can make themselves believe things which have no foundation in fact. The truth is, of course, that we can all let ourselves be led into believing something about another person which is inaccurate—even police officers, with all their training and caution, are sometimes fallible in that way.

It was the actions of Sidney Layfield which vividly reminded me of that human weakness. Sidney was a little man, barely five feet tall, and when I made his acquaintance upon my arrival at Aidensfield, he was well rounded in plump middle age. He had a round face, a very bald round head which shone in the morning sunshine, and yet in spite of his rotund outline, he was always neat and tidy. He wore tiny shoes and had tiny hands; I reasoned he must have been a very tiny child.

It was only because he was a resident of Aidensfield that I had become aware of him and his lifestyle—it is a police officer's job to know all about those who live and work on his patch for such local knowledge can sometimes enable a helping hand to be offered, advice to be given or a crime to be detected. I had never had cause to interview Sidney about anything, lawful or unlawful, and our social activities rarely coincided but because he and his wife, Mavis, lived in a modest terraced cottage in the village, I was aware of their existence.

Sidney, I learned over the course of a few months, had once been a stable lad and jockey; in his youth, he had been slim and lightweight, riding out at some of the local racing stables and even winning races both on the flat and over the sticks. But with increasing age and widening of his girth, he had given up his riding and now worked in the hardware department of a large store in Ashfordly. What had once been a slender figure with a thin face topped by lots of dark wavy hair, was now a chubby little chap who smoked a pipe and liked good food.

With the distinctive high-pitched voice

of a jockey, he drove a Morris Minor to work and appeared to live a very quiet and modest life. He rarely involved himself with village matters, other than an occasional visit to the pub for a couple of swift halves of bitter. At home, he read a lot, sitting in a comfortable armchair with his faithful pipe producing clouds of pungent smoke and if he had a hobby, it was horse-racing. He would sometimes have a modest bet on one of the classics, or on one of the local horses if it was running. Contentment seemed to be his mission in life and I was not surprised to learn that he had never been ambitious—his modest success at racing may have come from youthful determination, but as an adult, his mundane work at the hardware counter seemed to completely satisfy him. Whereas he might have been a champion jockey or highly successful trainer, he was now an expert on things like screws, tin tacks, woodworker's tools, frying pans and domestic tinware.

Mavis, his wife, however, was of a different mould. Not much taller than her husband, she'd had ambitions in her younger days—ambitions for Sidney that was, one of which was for Sidney to own, or at least manage, a thriving racing stable or to be a racehorse trainer, or to own his own shop or even be a manager of something, anything in fact. It was common knowledge around Aidensfield that she had often nagged at him in the hope he would stir himself into some kind of ambitious behaviour, but nothing had worked on Sidney. The stress of achieving professional success was not for him. He continued in his own sweet and undramatic world among knives, nails and nutcrackers, while Mavis ran cookery classes at the village hall (which my wife, Mary, attended).

Mavis also worked part-time during the summer months at a busy seaside café in Strensford. If Sidney had not wanted to find fame and fortune, it seemed that Mavis considered her own achievements to be a substitute—her renown as a meal maker was growing (Sidney's girth was evidence of that, we all felt). She had achieved a wide reputation as a fine cook through her successful cookery classes and also at the café where she produced mouth-watering dishes for the day-tripping masses. Her busy world seemed to take her mind off Sidney's lack of ambition, particularly during the summer when she spent long hours at the café, and that meant he had a respite from her constant efforts to thrust him into a more competitive world.

It must be said, though, that her efforts to stir him into bold action were less strenuous now. I think she realized he would never change—after all, he was approaching fifty. Sidney, instead of seeking opportunities to expand his horizons, happily occupied his spare time by taking his dogs for long walks. He had a pair of cocker spaniel bitches, one with black markings and the other with chestnut, and he walked miles with his dogs. At weekends, when Mavis was working, he would take a packed lunch and spend all day out on the moors and in the dales with Tinker and Bess. Probably as a legacy of his days working in racing stables, he rose very early each morning, often at 5.30 in the summer months, and he would get out of bed and take his dogs into Aidensfield Woods for a long walk before going to work.

As my own hours were irregular, with frequent patrols at dawn, I would sometimes see him paddling across the green towards the gate which led into the woods.

The woods were perfect for walking, especially when the sun was rising; in the spring, they were magical. They were deciduous woods comprised mainly of mature beech trees many of which had lovers' initials carved into their smooth grey trunks. There were other varieties too, such as sweet chestnuts, horse chestnuts, ash, oak, limes, elms, hollies and a wide range of conifers. The river ran its boulder-strewn course through the woods, producing waterfalls and deep pools of sufficient beauty to attract photographers and artists alike, and although the woods were owned and managed by Ashfordly Estate, there was no restriction on access to the public. The place was a network of fascinating footpaths providing everything from riverside walks to steep ascents to the heathery moors above.

I loved those woods and so did Sidney. In fact, the whole village loved them but Sidney's early morning visits managed to find places of solitude and quiet. Occasionally during my foot patrols, I would walk through the woods at dawn, chiefly as a deterrent to any lurking poachers, and from time to time had come across Sidney with his dogs. I discovered that one of his favourite places was Sally's Rock. This was a circular and rather flat boulder, something like a massive scone. It was positioned high above the river near Sally Foss which was one of the more beautiful of the waterfalls, and it provided wonderful views both upstream and downstream. Sidney would often sit there to smoke his pipe while his dogs galloped among the trees, exploring all manner of doggy delights. I'd seen him there several times, and he always waved his pipe in greeting. 'Now then, Constable,' he would call in his high-pitched voice. 'Nice to be out and about, eh?'

'Wonderful,' I would respond with feeling, and sometimes I'd pause for a chat or to make a fuss of Bess and Tinker.

'It's a shame I have to go to work!' he would sometimes add.

'I am at work!' I would laugh in response.

'Lucky for some,' he would reply without rancour.

Sidney's routine was just one of those things which I had mentally absorbed,

314

without any particular motive or intention, during my days at Aidensfield and his activities meant nothing to me until I chanced to see another person—a woman heading for the same woods in the early hours of the morning.

But that did not just happen on one occasion; during the summer months when the sun rose extremely bright and early, it became a regular event and it was soon noticed that her dawn excursions almost coincided with those of Sidney. I was one of several witnesses who came to realize that her trip to the wood occurred a few minutes after Sidney and dogs had vanished beneath the canopy of dark-green leaves.

The lady in question was Arabella Clarkson, a spinster of the parish of Aidensfield. In her early forties, Arabella was an artist who staged regular exhibitions in the district, and who taught part-time in Strensford Grammar School. A tall but very striking and pretty woman with long fair hair, dangling ear-rings and a slim figure, she wore long, flowing and highly colourful dresses and seemed to float about the place. Arabella was almost from another world; the sort of woman who would have made a fine model for a fairy had she been only six inches tall instead of nearly six feet. And most certainly, she was not known as an early riser.

She was the sort of lady who would remain in bed well into the middle of the morning if circumstances permitted, consequently this unexpected desire to rise at the crack of dawn and head for the woods was rather unusual. I found myself wondering whether she and Sidney met there; I wondered if he had found another love, someone to replace Mavis, and then I wondered what they must look like, Sidney and Arabella, walking side by side with him being knee high to a grasshopper and she towering like a maypole in its full array of colours. She was young and beautiful, he was middle-aged and balding; she was an artist, a person of individuality and ambition, while he was content to serve nuts and bolts from behind a dreary shop counter. Two opposites—but opposites can attract.

Even so, I kept telling myself, I had no evidence that they ever met in the woods nor did I know whether or not they emerged together. Apart from anything else, it was no business of mine, and I hoped it never would be. They were not committing a crime, even if they were meeting surreptitiously. Nonetheless, I did make a mental note of those occurrences, an instinctive reaction in a police officer, and I did note that they were never seen together in the village or elsewhere. Later, though, I saw that when Arabella was heading for the woods, she did not wear her gaudy clothes. She used dark green, brown or bronze outfits, sometimes trousers and sometimes skirts and blouses; furthermore, she began to carry an easel together with a case which held her brushes and paints. She had not done either of those things during the first of her visits. So was she painting? Or pretending to be painting? Was it a ploy to throw local gossips off the scent?

Her changed clothing was more like a camouflage now. For his walk, Sidney always wore old brown trousers and either a green or brown sweater on cool days or similarly coloured T-shirts when it was warmer. He'd always worn those for his morning walk but with that kind of colouring, it would be easy to hide oneself among the trees. I began to regard them as a very crafty couple. Ostensibly, and for public consumption, he had his dog walking to do, she had her painting—both rather neat and feasible excuses.

As is the case in such secretive liaisons, the entire village was soon agog with the notion that little Sidney Layfield was having an affair with Arabella. The only person who seemed unaware of the drama was Sidney's hard-working wife, chiefly because she spent long hours at work. The absence of Mavis during those months did seem to coincide with Sidney's meetings in the wood. People who were out and about in Aidensfield in the early morning noticed his daily trek accompanied by Tinker and Bess—the milkman, postman, some local lorry drivers, myself, farm and estate workers—all saw him heading for the gate which led into the wood and a few minutes later they saw Arabella floating towards the same destination. As most of the witnesses were men, there is little doubt that the esteem of Sidney rose greatly—none thought he was capable of such a thing, few reckoned he had the guts to defy or cheat Mavis. But the evidence suggested otherwise.

News of his infidelity did spread around Aidensfield as one would have expected and soon, people along the route of the couple's early morning walk through the village would themselves get out of bed, ostensibly to enjoy the early sunshine but in reality to watch Sidney and his dogs followed ten minutes later by Arabella and easel. It led to a good deal of tut-tutting in the post office-cum-village store, and quite a lot of speculation in the pub. Ladies gossiping in the shop wondered how long it would be before Mavis discovered the tryst and pondered her actions when she did find out, while drinkers in the pub speculated upon how Sidney coped with her height, her clothing and the uncomfortable floor of their woodland paradise.

It was one of Mavis's cookery-classes pupils who made a further contribution to the saga. There were no classes during the summer, of course, but one August day I was talking to Mrs Herringswell, the wife of a retired bank manager, when she chanced to mention Mavis. Mrs Herringswell, a big lady in the WI who was that year's speaker-finder, wanted to know whether I would talk about my work to the Aidensfield members sometime next January and when I agreed, she told me she was seeking other speakers and asked if I knew of anyone who was suitable. Without thinking about the aura which currently surrounded Sidney, I told her he might make a good speaker. I suggested he might tell them about his early days working with racehorses, something a world apart from making lace or decorating fruit cakes.

'Oh, Mr Rhea, how could you!' she expostulated. 'After what he's doing to Mavis, and just before their anniversary too!'

'Anniversary?' I puzzled.

'Yes, their wedding anniversary.'

'Really, when's that?' I asked.

'At the end of September. Poor Mavis is so excited about it,' she said. 'Twenty-five years, it's their silver wedding. And she knows nothing about his behaviour. There are times I wonder whether someone should alert her to the goings on with that artist woman.'

'I think not ...' I began.

'They think no one notices, with her dressing-up in camouflage like a soldier on manoeuvres. Sidney really ought to be ashamed of himself. At his age, too!'

'I've heard the rumours,' I chose my words with care, 'but there is no proof there is anything untoward going on.'

'Who needs proof?' she cried. 'Who needs proof when they parade themselves for all the world to see ... going off to the woods at sunrise like that, thinking nobody notices them ... we know what's going on, Mr Rhea, even if you don't.'

'Personal relationships like that are not a matter for the police.' I tried to be diplomatic. 'Furthermore, I don't think anyone should interfere. What goes on between Sidney and his wife is personal. And I still think he would make an interesting speaker.'

'Well, I'll think about your suggestion, of course, but I know my ladies, and I cannot see they would welcome an adulterer and wife-cheater into their midst. But I can see trouble brewing, Mr Rhea, mark my words. Sooner or later, Mavis Layfield is going to either find out or be told what's going on under the nose.'

She was right, of course. The pair were heading for trouble and one of the regular features of a police officer's life is to deal with fights between man and wife.

We call them domestics, a term meaning domestic and family disturbances. They are always unpleasant and there are no winners and losers—except for the unfortunate police officer who is called to quell the disturbance. He or she is always the loser because both protagonists turn against the peace-keeping constable as if the law is the cause of all the trouble and misbehaviour. It is not surprising that I had no wish to be called to a domestic involving Sidney and Mavis, should it ever happen.

I realised that Mrs Herringswell was speaking for the entire village. The rumours and innuendo which were flooding Aidensfield all tended to follow her line of thinking. I began to wonder if I should warn Sidney about his conduct and of the rumours he had sparked off—but then I told myself it was nothing to do with me. At that stage, there was no violence between him and Mavis, no outbreak of domestic friction, no throwing of either party out of the marital home or smashing of one another's belongings ... nothing in fact. Not even gloom on the face of Mavis as she went off to work or did her shopping in the village—she was behaving as if nothing was happening. In fact, at times she looked positively radiant.

And then two strange and rather surprising things happened.

Mary and I received an invitation to the

silver wedding celebrations of Sidney and Mavis. We were invited because Mary was a member of Mavis's cookery classes. The party would be in the form of a buffet supper with drinks and dancing, and it would be held in the ballroom of the Crown Hotel in Ashfordly on September 29th beginning at 8 p.m.

By the same post, we also received an invitation to the preview of an exhibition of new oil paintings by Arabella Clarkson. The preview was from 7 p.m. until 8 p.m. in the same ballroom of the Crown Hotel, Ashfordly, and at 8 p.m. the exhibition would be formally opened by—none other than Sidney Layfield! The exhibition would then continue for the following week. I must admit that, at first, I wondered how Mavis fitted into this scheme of things—it seemed Arabella and Sidney had concocted a fiendish scheme to be together. But to select his own silver wedding anniversary and to have his new woman there, albeit under the guise of supervising her preview of paintings, did seem rather ill-advised.

But the enigma thus presented did persuade everyone to go along, if only to find out what was really happening! Gossip around the village was, by this time, rife and those who had received invitations to this bizarre celebration were regarded as very honoured indeed. Not everyone had an invitation even though many would have loved to be there, but I did learn that Mrs Herringswell received one. Certainly, a lot of the ladies were determined to go, if only to see Mavis crown Arabella with a bottle of champagne or drench her with a plate of pea soup. It promised to be the social event of the decade.

On that Saturday night, Mary and I went along in our best clothes, having secured Mrs Quarry to baby-sit for our infants, and we arrived at 7 p.m. to see Arabella's preview of oil paintings. They were hanging around the walls of the ballroom, all numbered, and we received a small printed catalogue listing those on display.

Everyone received a free glass of sherry or a soft drink upon arrival and among the guests I noticed Mrs Herringswell and many other people from Aidensfield. It was while we wandered around the exhibition that I became aware of a large framed painting, still on its easel, on the stage at the far end. And it was covered with a green cloth. When I checked in the catalogue, it said, 'No. 77—to be unveiled by Sidney Layfield'.

Sidney! I felt he had recognition at last! But it was an enjoyable occasion and I reserved a painting of Aidensfield which depicted my house. Then at 8 p.m., Arabella in her most colourful and flowing of dresses, mounted the stage and was handed a microphone by a member of the hotel staff. She tapped it and tested it, and upon finding it was functioning correctly, called for silence. We all ceased our chatter and, like a good teacher, she drew us all closer to the stage. The painting was behind her, still under wraps, and then I saw Mavis and Sidney enter the stage from the right.

When everyone was silent, Arabella began to speak.

'Ladies and gentlemen, friends. Friends of mine and of Sidney and Mavis,' she started. 'I welcome you all and to thank you for coming to this preview. Previews are important to any artist and I hope you will persuade your friends to visit my exhibition from tomorrow. But tonight is more than a preview—in a moment, my preview becomes the silver wedding party for my friends, Mavis and Sidney. And as a special gesture, in a few minutes I am going to ask Sidney if he will unveil my most recent oil—this one behind me. But first, Mavis wants to say a few words.'

Mavis took the microphone, smiled at the gathering and said, 'I wanted to give Sidney a surprise for his silver wedding. I've always thought he should be more famous than he is,' and there was a ripple of good-natured laughter. We all knew what she meant. 'However, he would have none of it and so I had a word with Arabella. We knew he went into the woods for his morning walk and that he likes to sit for a while on Sally's Rock smoking that pipe of his while Tinker and Bess explore. And so Arabella has followed him for the last few months ... with her easel and paints and brushes. He had no idea she was watching him and certainly had no idea she was painting him, a little each day ... she behaved like a spy ... and I do know what the village was thinking ... but they were wrong! Sidney is not like that. And so, Sidney, if you will take hold of that cord and give it a gentle pull ...'

Arabella located the tip of the cord and passed it to him. With a puzzled frown on his face, he tugged the cord and the cover fell away to unveil a splendid portrait of himself. He was sitting on the rock smoking his faithful pipe. A small spiral of smoke rose from its bowl and behind were the trees and rock-strewn river while the foreground featured Bess and Tinker snuffling among the undergrowth ... and Sidney looked excellent. In fact, he looked majestic, handsome, strong and full of character. He stood back with shock and surprise on his face as everyone applauded—and then he hugged Mavis and Arabella, with tears in his eyes.

'I had no idea ...'

'It's for you,' said Arabella. 'Commissioned by your wife ...'

'Speech!' someone called from the floor and so Sidney took the microphone and in his squeaky but now emotional voice, said, 'I've been teased lately,' he said. 'Some of the chaps in the village have been asking what I was doing with Arabella in the woods ... well, now they know! It is a total surprise, ladies and gentlemen, I had no idea she was following me and painting me as I sat there thinking nice thoughts. But thank you, Arabella—and thank you, Mavis. Once again, thanks for this and for twenty-five lovely years. And now, I have a present for you ... I was going to give it to you later, but, well, perhaps now is the right moment.'

He went behind the curtains and produced another painting, this time smaller than his own, but covered with a cloth. He passed it to Mavis who took it, opened it and found a portrait of herself as a young woman. She was standing at a farmhouse table full of pastry and cooking utensils, a real country scene.

'Great minds think alike,' he grinned as he kissed her. 'And it was painted by Arabella—from photographs. I had the devil's own job to stop you finding out I'd taken photographs from the album!'

'It's wonderful,' said Mavis, hugging the little fellow.

'It's been a hectic few months!' sighed Arabella. 'Especially keeping two big secrets ...'

As the applause died away, we all adjourned to the food tables which were being uncovered by the hotel staff for the wedding anniversary celebrations were about to commence. As the principals left the stage, a three-piece orchestra moved on and began to prepare to play for dancing.

As I moved towards the food, Mrs

Herringswell appeared at my shoulder and said, 'Mr Rhea, I think I might ask Mr Layfield if he would speak to us after all.'

'And Arabella?' I suggested.

'Yes,' she said smiling. 'And Arabella. They really surprised everyone, didn't they?'

Later, I realized just how rumours and disinformation can circulate due to a series of misinterpreted actions. The people of Aidensfield had placed their own salacious interpretation upon a series of innocent events and had come to believe what they wanted to believe. And I was no better. As a policeman, I should have not made such assumptions but then, as I entered Aidensfield Wood one fine autumn morning for a walk, I was reminded of Sidney's pipe and of the smoke captured so atmospherically in Arabella's splendid painting.

For some reason, the words of an old saying came to mind. It was 'There is no smoke without fire.'

Oddly enough, it was the same stretch of woodland which featured in another case where speculation was allowed to outstrip the facts of an incident. In this instance, it featured an elderly widow called Edna Waggett. She lived in a beautiful if neglected detached house of mellow limestone set on a lovely hillside site. Close to the centre of Aidensfield, it had been her family home for more than eighty-five years. She had been born there and had lived there ever since, her husband living with her in this spacious home upon their marriage.

He was a salesman of cattle medicines who had died some ten years before my arrival, but between them, they had produced five sons all of whom lived away from Aidensfield. One was in South Africa, another in Mexico, two in the Midlands and the nearest in Cumberland; all had been successful in their chosen careers but their work and the distance from Aidensfield meant they rarely visited her at home. She did, however, go and see them from time to time, and had been to South Africa twice since reaching eighty. She had also spent a month with her son in Mexico for her eightieth birthday. Edna was a remarkable lady who managed to look after herself; I had never known her bc ill or incapacitated, and she attributed

330

her spritely condition to a daily nip of whisky before going to bed coupled with the ability to get a good night's sleep.

As with all the aged and infirm in the villages on my patch, I kept a discreet eye on Edna, sometimes popping in if I didn't see her lights on during a dark evening, or if the milk or papers were late in being collected from her doorstep. She always received me with a smile and an appreciation of my concern, but inevitably said she was quite well, thank you, and I hadn't to worry myself about her. But then one dark and chilly Wednesday evening in autumn, I saw her wandering along the main street dressed only in a light blouse and skirt. It was cold enough to warrant a sweater at least or even an overcoat and she looked so vulnerable. I stopped for a chat.

'Hello, Edna,' I always used her Christian name, as indeed everyone did. For some reason she disliked the formality of being called Mrs Waggett. 'Where are you going?'

'I'm going to see if my grandma is all right,' she smiled sweetly. 'I always go and see her on a Thursday night.'

'Your grandma?' For a moment I was

flummoxed by her response and then realized she had regressed to her past. Old people did this from time to time, and I knew the only way to deal with her was to humour her.

'Where's she live?' I asked.

'At Beckside Cottage.' She looked at me as if I should know that. 'She's always lived here.'

'She's gone out,' I answered. 'She asked me to let you know. Maybe you could call another day?'

'Oh, all right,' she smiled sweetly. 'But I always go on Thursdays.'

'It's Wednesday today,' I countered. 'Come along, I'll walk you home.'

'Is it Wednesday?' she puzzled. 'I thought it was Thursday, Mr Rhea. Shall I go tomorrow, then?'

'Yes,' I went along with her illusion. 'I think that would be a good idea.' I returned her to the house and advised her to lock the door when I left but a week later, I found her again, this time carrying an empty bucket.

'Hello, Edna,' I said. 'Where are you off to now?'

'To the pump, to get some water for my washing,' she smiled. 'It's wash day tomorrow, you know, and I have a lot to do so I want an early start.'

'The pump's not working,' I tried to persuade her. 'There's a blockage of some kind. Come along, I'll take you home and see if we can find water somewhere else.'

By the time we reached her house, she had reverted to the present day and seemed quite astonished that I should want to help her fill her bucket.

'There's nothing wrong with my taps,' she snapped when I reminded her I was going to help her. 'And I have hot water laid on!'

In the week that followed, I came across her wandering off to the dairy to get some cheese (the dairy had closed before World War II); off to visit relations such as her father in his butcher's shop or aunts, uncles, grandparents and friends, all of whom had died many years earlier; off to buy some new candles ready for the winter when an electric light bulb had blown, off to the fields to help a long-dead farmer with his haytime; off to the Methodist chapel for a service when it had closed several years ago; off to the blackmith's shop to bring the horse home after being shod and off to the railway station to meet her husband after a business trip to Glasgow.

During my patrols around Aidensfield, I encountered others who had found Edna wandering about in a state of some bewilderment, invariably having regressed to her childhood or her young married days, The district nurse, Margot Horsefield, promised to keep an eye on her as did the postman, milkman, local shopkeepers and others who noticed the passing scene in Aidensfield. Each of them had found poor Edna wandering about in a state of some distress, invariably seeking something or someone from her past life.

It was evident she needed help and I decided it was a matter for the family so I rang one of her sons. I selected Alan because he lived nearest; his home was at Penrith on the edge of the Lake District and I think he was manager of a slate quarry.

'Thanks, Mr Rhea,' he said on the phone. 'Some friends in Aidensfield have also told us about her behaviour. My wife and I were coming to stay with her this coming weekend, to try and decide what to do with her. She is expecting us on Saturday morning, I said we'd be there for dinner. Maybe I could pop in sometime for a chat about her?'

'Yes, of course,' I welcomed the opportunity.

Between that day and the following weekend, she wandered off several more times, on each occasion being found by a resident of Aidensfield and returned to her house. It emerged, though, that when being taken home, she would snap out of her imaginary world and revert to the present day. The fact that she had imagined herself in the past was upsetting for her and one day I found her in tears. She was standing outside her back door, one hand on the door jamb and weeping softly.

'Edna?' I touched her on her shoulder. 'What's wrong?'

'Oh, I don't know, Mr Rhea. Senility, I think. Old age. Daftness ... I find myself standing in the street or outside my dad's old shop and not knowing how I got there or why I am there, then somebody says I'd told them I was off to see my mother or visit my granny ... and they've been dead years, Mr Rhea. I must be going daft. It worries me, I am all right, you know, really. I'm not senile, am I? I can

335

look after myself and do my own cooking and cleaning. I'm not really going barmy, am I? I don't want to be a burden to anyone ...'

'Alan's coming to see you, isn't he?' I said. 'On Saturday. He'll look after you ...'

'Yes, he's good to me is our Alan. And Laura, that's his wife. A lovely woman, very good for him she's been. But I don't want to go away, I don't want to live with them, I'd be a burden, you know ... he has his own life, you see.'

'I am sure he will do all he can for you.'

'My own mother used to wander, you know. We would find her all over the place, down the fields looking for her father who'd been dead for years ... that sort of thing.'

'But you've got your health and strength,' I tried to reassure her as I led her indoors, sat her down and made her a cup of tea. I found some cakes in the pantry and we had a pleasant talk beside her fire. I told her that the whole village would look after her, that she was not going senile or losing her senses and that we all admired the way she kept herself neat and tidy, and how she maintained her sturdy independence. I felt sure there would be no need for her to move to another place—I wondered if she feared an old folks' home. She listened and smiled at me from time to time, but I could see that memories of her recent experiences were weighing on her mind. The experiences with her own mother, of which I knew very little because they had happened years ago, clearly upset Edna because she recalled them every time she switched back from her regression into the current time.

I passed word of Alan's impending arrival around those villagers who had been directly involved with Edna and that eased our minds somewhat. On the Thursday and Friday, Edna went through a tearful few hours, telling her friends and neighbours that she thought she was becoming mentally ill.

They reassured her and suddenly she would switch out of that mood and become the Edna we all knew—or the Edna we had known until her current condition had manifested itself. But for us all, Saturday—and Alan—could not come soon enough.

But on that Saturday morning, Edna vanished.

The alarm was raised by Ted Fryer, the butcher. Ted now occupied the shop which Edna's father had owned; it was a thriving business with much of its success being due to Edna's late father, Dick Farrell. And now, after the passage of many years, Ted continued in the same tradition. Every Tuesday and Saturday morning he toured Aidensfield and district in his delivery van, taking orders and delivering to his customers. Being the daughter of the man who had founded the business in Aidensfield, Edna was one of Ted's special customers. Every Saturday, she took delivery of a modest joint of beef for the weekend along with other things to last her until he called again on Tuesday, such as bacon, some lamb chops and sausages. But that Saturday morning her kitchen door had been standing wide open; he had shouted into the house as he always did but had got no reply. Knowing of Edna's recent propensity for wandering, he'd entered the house shouting into every room, including upstairs, but in every case had not received a response. A quick search of her garden, a few enquiries of neighbours and a quick visit to the post office were enough to convince him that she'd wandered off once more. Just to be sure, though, and prior to calling me, he had returned to her house for a final check, shouting into the bathroom and the outside toilet.

The kitchen door was still standing wide open but there was no sign of her and then he noticed a certain knife was missing.

'It was a knife her father used years ago,' he said. 'I think it had been a present from her father's father, when he started off with his business. She kept it as sharp as a razor, just like he always did. Her dad would test it by shaving hairs off his arms; she always said his knives were the sharpest and best-kept for miles around. Then when he died, she inherited it. She used it for carving her Sunday joint. I know the knife well because she asks me to sharpen it once in a while, she says nobody can sharpen a knife like a butcher can. Her dad was noted for his knives, and she asked me to look after that one. I sharpened it and cleaned it. She thought a lot about it, Mr Rhea, a family treasure. It always hung on a hook over the draining board; it had a hole in the handle with a bit of string through it.

But it's gone. She'd never part with that knife, Mr Rhea. Never.'

'You mean she's taken it with her?' At first, the implication of that remark did not fully sink into my mind.

'I did have a look around, Mr Rhea, in the washing-up bowl and knife drawer ... it's not there.'

Ted knew, as I did, that in recent weeks Edna had been showing signs of insecurity and depression and I began to understand the import of his words.

'She's not likely to harm herself, is she?' I put to him.

'Well, she hasn't been right, has she? She's been saying she doesn't want to be a burden, she's been worrying about losing her mind, that sort of thing.'

'But she's too sensible to do anything daft!' I said.

'Things have been getting to her and I wouldn't say she's been very sensible in recent times,' he shook his head sagely. 'But whatever, Mr Rhea, I reckon we ought to be looking for her.'

'So do I,' I heard myself say. 'Right, I need help, people to search all the places she might visit, all her old haunts ...'

'But if she's taken a knife, Mr Rhea,

340

she'll likely go somewhere away from her old haunts.'

'I wonder how long she's been gone?' I was speaking aloud. 'Look, Ted, I'll ask around the village before I mount a massive search party. Somebody must have seen her wandering off.'

'Right, you do that, and I'll ring round a few of the blokes I know to get a search party organized. The cricket team'll turn out for one thing, and there's plenty of kids off school this morning to give a helping hand.'

'Right, Ted, thanks. I'll do a quick recce around the village, and then go back to my house to ring for assistance. Can you see me at my house in, say, forty-five minutes?'

'Right,' he agreed.

The trouble with a Saturday morning is that the village does not follow the same pattern of activity as it does from Monday to Friday and one consequence was that no one had seen Edna that morning. People who went to work or came into the village during the week, did not do so on a Saturday.

After half-an-hour's frantic questioning in the centre of Aidensfield, I produced no news of Edna. I returned to my police house and telephoned Sergeant Blaketon at Ashfordly.

'There's me and PC Ventress on duty here,' he said. 'We'll be there in fifteen minutes. I can leave PC Foxton to man the office.'

'I'll wait at my police house,' I said. 'I've some volunteers meeting me there.'

And so a search party for Edna was organized. While I was awaiting the arrival of my various colleagues and volunteers, I rang several contacts in Aidensfield to ask if they'd seen Edna going walkabout. None had. We were no further forward and after pondering her recent mental state, I must admit I was bothered about her. Within three-quarters of an hour, Sergeant Blaketon and PC Alf Ventress had arrived, along with Ted Fryer and his team of villagers. I described Edna to them all and outlined her recent behaviour, reminding the local people of her past family contacts, places she might have gone to visit in a state of regression. We divided the volunteers into teams of four and set them each the task of searching a particular area of Aidensfield, some using motor vehicles to reach the outlying portions, others using sticks to search the moorland and rough vegetation and yet more to concentrate on buildings and likely hiding places within the village—places like the churches, village hall and outbuildings would be searched. We agreed to meet again in two hours at the police house, i.e. at one o'clock lunchtime. While Sergeant Blaketon and Alf Ventress concentrated on buildings within the village, I had to make enquiries along the routes she might have taken to leave the security of Aidensfield.

People washing their pots or shaking their mats might have seen her wandering past. And I was lucky. I knocked on the door of the last house in the village along the road to Briggsby and a young woman answered. She was Susan Pennington who said she'd seen Edna walking briskly past her house shortly after nine this morning, heading for Aidensfield Woods. I asked whether Edna was clutching anything, but Susan hadn't noticed anything in her hands, although Edna had been dressed for a hot summer day rather than a cool and rather damp autumn morning. Before organizing a large search of the woods, I needed more confirmation that Edna was in there and remembered Sidney Layfield's morning walks with the spaniels. I hurried to his home and asked if he'd seen her.

'Oh, yes, Mr Rhea,' he said. 'I saw the old lady and passed the time of day with her. She said she was going to meet up with her husband in the wood. She said she hadn't seen him for a long time and wanted to be with him. I thought it was a bit funny, I'd not seen any old gentleman in there.'

I groaned at that comment and asked, 'Was she carrying anything?'

He shook his head. 'Coat you mean? Handbag? No, nothing, she was bare-armed too, a bit on the chilly side for that. And damp too.'

I explained that she was wandering and that her mind was not functioning as it should be, whereupon Sidney said he would join the search, along with his dogs. He and they knew the woods intimately. Satisfied that she had wandered into the woods and that her disappearance had all the hallmarks of a potential suicide attempt, I hurried back to locate Ted and his volunteers.

Next I radioed Sergeant Blaketon in his car. The outcome was that the search would now be concentrated upon

Aidensfield Woods. I had a map of the woods at my house and hurried to locate it, then we all assembled near the war memorial to be allocated an area of the wood. I explained about her words to Sidney Layfield, about the knife and about her state of mind and, after due warning from Sergeant Blaketon to keep well away from the knife if she started to wave it about, we sallied forth.

I was in the same party as Sidney and our route took us towards the western heights of the wood, the part where the myriad paths wandered among the boulders and beeches below the cliff face which reached to the heathery moor above. It was a rugged area, rough being perhaps a more apt description but it was Sidney who noticed the footprints in the damp earth as we came to a junction.

'Fresh prints, Mr Rhea,' he said. 'A woman's shoe, by the look of it ... heading that way.' And he pointed.

'Come on,' I said.

It is sufficient to say that a few minutes later, I found Edna. With Sidney and his dogs panting behind me, I came across her sitting on a tree stump beneath a huge beech tree. She had the butcher's knife clutched in her two fists, its point reaching to the sky. She appeared to be staring with high concentration at the knife but she was unharmed. When I approached, she smiled and said, 'Hello, Mr Rhea. How nice to see you. And who is the gentleman with you? What nice dogs ...'

'That is Mr Layfield with his spaniels, he knows these woods very well, Edna. We have come to take you home. Now, can I have the knife?'

'No, you cannot, Mr Rhea! That is a very special knife, a family heirloom. You cannot have it, most certainly not. It is mine—and I am using it!'

'No, Edna, you must not use it ... you must give it to me ... or place it on the ground and then let me come for you ...'

I held back during this dialogue, not wishing to alarm and anger her because the point of the knife was dangerously close to her exposed throat and breast.

'Mr Rhea.' She looked at me coldly and with determination. 'You have no right to interfere in this. I am doing this for me and my dear husband, Henry. We used to come here, you see, to be alone, to be together. I want to be with him now which is why I have come here.'

At this point, I was uncertain whether she had regressed to former times or was speaking of the present time. But the scenario had a feel of urgency and desperation about it. With only little Sidney present, I wondered what on earth I could do to prevent her using the knife, or how I could cope if she did use it ... talking seemed to be the only answer.

'Edna, please. Give me the knife.'

'Mr Rhea, I have made my decision quite clear to you. The knife is mine, a family treasure, it belonged to my father. You cannot have it. I refuse, Mr Rhea, totally. Now, if you will leave me in peace, I shall prepare to meet my dear husband ... Henry, did you know Henry, Mr Rhea?'

'No, I'm afraid not. I haven't been at Aidensfield all that long.'

'A shame, Mr Rhea, a dreadful shame. He was a wonderful man, Mr Rhea, and the finest of husbands ... I used to meet him here, beneath this tree, all those years ago.'

'You loved him?' I had to keep her talking until the others arrived. I hoped Sidney would use his initiative to go for the others who were somewhere among the trees but could not ask him outright.

'He was a source of strength and help to me,' she said.

'We could all do with some help,' I said, turning to look at Sidney and this time he understood my message.

'I'll go, now that Mrs Waggett is safe,' he said and I knew by the expression on his face that he would fetch Blaketon and the others.

'And you need not remain here, Constable Rhea,' she said. 'I am quite happy, quite safe. I want to remember Henry, that is all. Then I shall go home.'

As little Sidney walked away with his spaniels, Edna watched him leave and then, placing the knife on the tree stump, she struggled to her feet. I was tempted to rush in and seize the knife, but in a flash, she had it in her right hand as she made for the back of the huge trunk. She moved swiftly behind the tree, the knife glistening in the shafts of sunlight which filtered through the canopy of leaves above as I ran towards her. But as I reached the rear of the tree trunk, she was already standing close to it, her face wreathed in concentration as she picked out a heart and two sets of initials which had been carved into the trunk a long, long time ago.

'Henry carved this for me,' she said softly, the tip of the knife chipping at the tough grey bark. 'Our initials, you see, Mr Rhea. And a heart. A love token. I thought it was time I renewed it. Do you mind? I do hope you are not going to try and remove my knife before I get the job finished.'

'No,' I said. And now I understood. We had misunderstood her motives all along! This was her way of reuniting herself with Henry but as I watched for a few moments as she chipped away at the wood, I did not know whether she thought she was operating in times past, or whether she was in the present.

Deciding not to suggest to her that we had worried about a possible suicide attempt, I sat down on the tree stump to await the completion of her task, and, with some trepidation, the arrival of Sergeant Blaketon and his team of volunteers.

This Large Print Book for the Partially sighted, who cannot read normal print, is published under the auspices of

THE ULVERSCROFT FOUNDATION